The Serpent of Senargad

Under the spell of the evil Rhymester the once
peaceful kingdom of Senargad has become a place
of fear, death and destruction. Battles rage, the
savage Wolf-Guard roam the country and, in
subterranean caverns, prisoners are held captive by
the terrible Serpent of Senargad. It seems that no
one can defeat the Rhymester . . .

This is the fifth story in the Pangur Bán series.
The other titles (in order) are: *Shape-Shifter, Pangur
Bán, the White Cat, Finnglas of the Horses* and
Finnglas and the Stones of Choosing.

Fay Sampson is the author of eighteen books
for children and teenagers. She is a full-time writer,
and lives with her husband in a centuries-old Devon
cottage, overlooking Dartmoor. Her favourite
occupation is researching the Celtic times in which
the book is set.

To Paula Pat

the Serpent of Senargad

FAY SAMPSON

To Moira

Happy Reading!

Fay Sampson

A LION PAPERBACK

Oxford · Batavia · Sydney

Copyright © 1989 Fay Sampson

Published by
Lion Publishing plc
Sandy Lane West, Littlemore, Oxford, England
ISBN 0 7459 1520 5
Lion Publishing Corporation
1705 Hubbard Avenue, Batavia, Illinois 60510, USA
ISBN 0 7459 1520 5
Albatross Books Pty Ltd
PO Box 320, Sutherland, NSW 2232, Australia
ISBN 0 7324 0027 9

First edition 1989

Printed and bound in Great Britain
by Cox and Wyman Ltd, Reading

Part 1

1

Finnglas shouted defiance at the grey king Jarlath of the Northlands.

'Never! I will not wed you!'

A shudder of horror ran round the hall. The Wolf-Guard in their hairy cloaks, the women of the court in their embroidered dresses, the king's only daughter Kara, even the gold-clad king himself started in amazement. No one denied Jarlath of the Wolves what he wanted, unless there was something they valued more than life.

Kara's eyes grew wide as she watched the other girl. This filthy, ragged slip of a foreigner, who claimed she was an Irish princess, who said she had sailed here only to beg corn for the starving. Could anyone believe such insolence? Yet the girl plainly had courage.

The other prisoner, a burly young monk in a stained brown robe, moved closer to her. But what had happened to the third prisoner, the white cat?

In the whole hall only one hooded figure stood unmoved, with the stillness of an icicle. The king's own shadow, greyer than the king himself, who shaped the king's will and wove the king's thought. More feared than Jarlath himself. The Rhymester.

That shadow moved now. One long, black-nailed finger pointed at Finnglas. Her face was pale under the salt-air tan, but she did not flinch. Not though the threats and curses were mounting about her like an evil storm, before which she was helpless.

Kara gazed at her with a mixture of disgust and astonishment. She herself was a real princess. She slept in a golden bed, on pillows of silk, covered with blankets of softest, fleecy wool. Her skin was fair and smooth, protected from wind and sun. Her hair was braided with jewels. Her scarlet skirt was embroidered with pure gold, her jacket woven from it, and round her neck hung a collar of silver and coral.

But she had to admit, grudgingly, that this dirty, thieving pirate who called herself Finnglas had at least the pride of a princess. You did not need to decipher the six colours of her tartan cloak to see that she must indeed have been royally reared. She had stolen the king's golden ship. Found it floating empty, she claimed! She called herself a follower of the Dolphin Arthmael, who, everyone knew, was the enemy of the Kingdom of the Wolves. And now, even now that she was their prisoner, she refused to take her only chance of life and freedom. She would not marry the widowed Jarlath and join her father's kingdom of the Summer Isle to the golden-gated city of Senargad.

The end could not be long. She would be made to understand. The chilling words issued from the Rhymester's mouth like the harsh breath of winter that freezes instantly into drops of ice.

'From the bitter hills and the cruel snow,
Dealing death I make them go.
Up from the dark, loosed from my thrall,
I raise the Wolf-Guard in this hall!'

Knowing what was going to happen, Kara could not restrain the movement of fear that sent her hands half-way to her eyes. But she was Jarlath's daughter, though he did not love her. She fought the impulse down. All round her the women were shrieking, covering their faces, turning away, running into the furthest corners of the hall. Kara forced herself to stand her ground and watch.

The soldiers lunged forward. For a brief moment there was a mass of thrusting helmets and flying cloaks. Then there were no more faces of men. Only the snarling, black-lipped muzzles of wolves, sharp-pricked ears, straining legs and tails, and a baying roar that made the rafters tremble.

8

The Irish princess disappeared under the leaping tide. Her monk-companion, Niall, shouted in anguish. With a gesture of contempt the Rhymester gave the command that brought the Wolf-Guard cowering down. Ears flattened, muscles quivering, they crouched before the lash of his tongue.

Niall picked the princess up and folded her in his arms. She was trembling with shock. This time Kara could not find it in her heart to despise this Finnglas. Even now, in her terror, she had not given in. But she must soon. The wolves were restive still, licking their dribbling lips. Their manhood was only just in the Rhymester's control, their wolf-souls fighting for possession.

Then one wolf at the back of the hall turned. Grey ears stiffened. He sprang erect, growling horribly at the half-open door. In the space beyond Kara had a fleeting vision as of a very small ghost. A tiny, triangular, terrified face. A piteous pink mew. The whisk of a once-white tail. The third, forgotten, prisoner, now a prisoner no more. A half-starved, soot-smudged cat took to his heels and fled out of the palace.

'Pangur Bán!' cried Niall and Finnglas.

With a howl of rage, the pack swept after him. In vain the Rhymester's spell screamed out behind them. It trapped the rearguard, but the rest were gone, beyond the reach of his voice. Pandemonium broke out in the courtyard. Claws scrabbling over paving-stones, tearing at wooden walls, throats raging for the kill.

'Imprison these two in the tower and guard them securely,' grated Jarlath. 'Tomorrow she weds me.'

'No! No!'

As the remaining wolves leaped to seize Finnglas, Niall dashed to stop them. Kara gasped. But there could only be one end. The teeth of the nearest wolf gripped his raised arm before he had time to strike. It growled greedily. The king's lips stretched in a mirthless smile of victory.

The young monk was silent, sweat trickling down his face from his half-shaven head. But his free arm was firm about

9

the still-protesting princess as the last of the wolves flowed menacingly around them and steered them to a dark door in a stone-based tower.

The hall was almost empty now, the women fluttering like a field of poppies bruised by hail. The Rhymester had withdrawn within his hood, the burning red of his eyes no longer visible. Only the gold-cloaked king stood on the edge of the dais, his fists gripping white, and his face once more coldly dark as the Arctic sea in January.

Kara saw that look, and a chill gripped her own stomach. At any moment her father's anger would be turned on her.

2

Still clutching her dignity about her, Kara slipped from the hall as hastily as she could. There was, after all, a great deal to be done if her father insisted on the wedding-feast tomorrow.

She stalked about the palace, causing panic in the kitchen and consternation among the chambermaids. There was food to be prepared that should have taken a week. There were rooms to be made ready, guests to be invited. And clothes. Everything that Finnglas was wearing must surely be burned.

Kara chose the garments herself, fit for a bride. A silken underslip. A white blouse, rich with embroidery. A flowing skirt. Fur-lined slippers to replace those dreadful boots that Finnglas wore. Then jewelry. As she piled riches into the arms of her waiting-women, their eyes grew rounder.

'All these?' said Elli. 'For *her*?'

'I am a king's daughter,' answered Kara haughtily. 'A royal princess of Senargad. Would you have that Irish vagabond think we cannot afford such wedding-gifts?'

'No. Of course not, your Highness.'

Elli's eyelashes fell, for she was never bold. She knew her mistress spoke from pride. Jarlath was rich indeed, but never rich enough. Why else had his eyes flashed with fire when he found he had captured Finnglas, princess of the Summer Isle? Why else did he want to marry her? To bind the fairy gold mines of her father in the south to his gold-hungry kingdom of the north.

The chattering women crossed the yard with their arms full of finery to dress Finnglas when they had washed her. Kara walked behind them. Dusk was falling early as the harvest wagons came rolling down into the city. Dark

11

storm-clouds were massing on the hills. Soon winter would hold them all in its icy grip.

She started suddenly as a deep voice rang out across the gold-lit twilight.

'Oh, give thanks to the Lord, for he is good.
For his steadfast love endures for ever.'

She stood incredulous and shocked. That impudent monk Niall was singing from the window of the tower, as though he had nothing to fear. In the yard below wolves bristled and snarled. They guarded every corner, every doorway. Still four-footed, fanged, under the grey Rhymester's thrall. There could be no escape. Tomorrow Finnglas would be queen.

Queen. A small familiar pain twisted at Kara's heart. She had never known her mother. Jarlath's young bride had died three hours after her daughter was born. After that, the king could hardly look on Kara without hate. They said it was then that the Rhymester entered the palace. But tomorrow there would be a new queen to take her mother's place.

She made herself go up the tower stairs to face Finnglas.

Even before she reached the last turn she could hear the other girl protesting.

'Skirts! Slippers! I am a seafarer, not a fine court lady! I follow the Dolphin Arthmael.'

Finnglas stood facing the doorway. Green fire flashed from her hazel eyes. They had dressed her like a princess now in the richly-embroidered clothes. The women were trying to brush the tangles from her hair and holding up jewels against her wind-browned skin.

Kara looked at her coldly. 'That Dolphin you speak of, whom the ignorant here call Lok the Lucky, is banished from these waters by my father's orders. He may not approach the coasts of Senargad on pain of death. Outside these walls he must not even be named.'

To her amazement the girl burst out laughing.

'Arthmael cannot be killed! Once he did die, and now there is no more death.'

How could she laugh like that, so freely and merrily, standing in a prison tower, ringed by wolves, from which there was no escape?

'You will see!' Kara snapped. 'You will obey my father or die tomorrow. Your Dolphin cannot save you here.'

And she turned on her heel, her heart hammering furiously, and marched back to her own room.

Thunder rumbled round the walls. The women were coming back from the tower. There was an almost inaudible scraping at Kara's chamber door. Elli came in. How tiresome she was, with her timid, apologetic ways.

'I'm sorry if I'm disturbing you, your Highness,' she said. 'But do you want me to help you get ready for bed? It's . . . '

The words were drowned in a sudden baying from outside that sent the colour flying from Elli's round cheeks. Kara spun back to the window. She was just in time to see something small, something swift, something white whisking out of the palace gates into the town with the wolf-pack charging after it.

'It's that disgusting cat again!' she cried. 'That friend of thieves. I hope they tear him limb from limb.'

'I don't,' whispered Elli to herself. 'Poor little thing. I pray Pangur Bán gets away.'

Next moment, the storm broke above Senargad. Rain lashed down, curtaining the hills, sluicing down the walls, bouncing off the paving stones in an angry spray. The howling of the hunt was lost in the drumming downpour. Those wolves that remained slunk under the pelting eaves with sodden fur.

Hours later Kara lay awake listening to the sky weeping the tears she could not shed. Across the foot of her bed Elli lay snoring gently. Suddenly the palace was in tumult again. Voices yelling, torches flashing red in the darkness. The horrible howling of wolves.

'What is it, your Highness! Are we being attacked? Will we be burned in our beds?'

13

The terrified Elli was clutching her princess by the sleeve. Kara shook her off.

'Leave go of me, you wretch. Let me go and see.'

She seized a candle and started down the stairs.

'No, your Highness!'

But Elli followed her, quaking, too scared to be left alone.

Kara reached the first landing. Two wolves sprang out, teeth bared. Even Kara gasped before she could stop herself. But they recognized her and let her pass, though their eyes still raged dangerously. Slaves, wolves, warriors were running in all directions, in and out of the teeming rain and the flaring torchlight. Kara made herself stride through them with her chin defiantly raised, to make it seem she was not afraid. At the door of the great hall she halted. Her father's voice was rising ominously, but more dangerous still was the silent shadow of the Rhymester behind him.

'*Well*, Braggi? What is this you have come to confess to me now?'

'It was a trick, your Majesty. A lying trick,' the Chief Wolf whined. 'Some traitor . . . '

'Do not dare to suggest that you have failed your duty a second time. What is the meaning of this uproar in my palace?'

The grey tail curved between trembling hind legs. The wolf crouched lower on its quivering belly. Then, hideously, it rolled over on its back, waving its legs in the air in abject submission.

'They . . . they seem to have escaped, your Majesty.'

'*Escaped! Who* has escaped?'

'A . . . all three, great Sire. The cat Pangur Bán, the monk Niall and . . . the princess Finnglas! It seems there was a boy . . . '

Even as he spoke the wolf was on his feet, cowering, slobbering, backing away into the doorway where Kara stood.

'*What!*' The hooded figure behind the king rose higher than ever.

'The guard are searching for them, your Majesty. We'll find them, we'll drag them back, we'll torture the traitor.'

'*Get out!*' Jarlath was coming down the hall like a rising whirlwind, gold-edged cloak spinning about him, grey hair streaming. 'Restore her to me, or I'll turn you all into rotting crow's meat!'

The wolf fled, claws scrabbling on wet stone. The king was facing his daughter. His cold grey eyes burned now red as the Rhymester's. He seemed to stare right through her. The words hissed like handfuls of snow on a raging fire.

'By Hel! I'll catch the traitors! I'll have revenge.'

He turned, and the Rhymester's greater shadow moved in his shadow, guiding him angry step by angry step.

3

They had gone. Pangur Bán, Niall, Finnglas. The cat, the monk and the girl, taking with them the king's gold ship loaded with the king's own corn. Someone had set them free. The sunshine sparkled on the wet earth and the blue sky laughed.

Everyone in the palace of Senargad, from the noblest earl to the youngest slave, was in a state of terror. Kara had to summon all her courage to pour her father's breakfast ale with a hand that scarcely trembled. A few cowed wolves slunk about the court, snarling at anyone who crossed their path. The rest had set out in pursuit. Like the watchful wolves the Rhymester prowled with restless, menacing strides. He passed the golden gates and scowled at the sea. He leaned from the highest window of the tower, muttering to the sky. The sound of threatening chants throbbed from his darkened room and evil-smelling smoke crept under the door.

The news grew blacker by the hour. The pursuing long-ships had been wrecked by whales, the sea-wolves drowned or cast away. Arthmael, the great scarred Dolphin, had re-appeared, leaping and laughing in the face of all danger. The prisoners had flown beyond the reach of Jarlath, south towards the Summer Isle.

The hour of the king's wedding-feast approached. The terrified cooks did not know what to do. They could not prevent the smell of roasting meat and baking pies drifting across the yard to the king's nostrils. The roads to Senargad were dark with horses. Jarlath's noble neighbours, their wives, their retinues, were obeying the hasty summons to attend his marriage. Peasant girls had brought garlands of flowers from the countryside and heaped them in the hall, with a corn-dolly to hang over Finnglas's wedding-bed. Kara whispered to her women that they must carry them outside. They started to steal from the hall with their arms full of flowers.

The king's face grew dark with rage. His fist crashed down upon the oaken table making the golden goblets dance.

'By the Great Wolf Fenrir! There shall be a marriage here! I will not be mocked. You, Kara, daughter that never brought me any joy. If I have lost one kingdom, you shall bring me another. You skulking messengers, run! Take this word to King Thidrandi of Bergenring. My daughter here will wed his son, Prince Oslaf, before three days are out.'

'No!' A little despairing gasp escaped from Kara.

'*No?*' The king started to rise, towering over his daughter.

A chill entered the room. The Rhymester stood behind him, watching her with glowing eyes from under his hood.

Kara's lips were stiff with fear, choking back her protest. Oslaf. Heir to that land of black-leaved forests and ice-tipped mountains. Oslaf, who was kept in a cold castle by a bottomless fiord. Oslaf, born vacant and witless, with pale blue eyes and drooling mouth. So the dreadful day had come. She must wed him at last.

The two children had been betrothed in their cradles. Two golden-haired babies bearing promise of harder gold. Growing apart. Proud, clever Kara in the wolf-kingdom on the wind-swept sands of Senargad. The smiling idiot Oslaf, hidden in the forest fastness of the mountains of Bergenring.

'That poor little boy,' whispered soft-hearted Elli.

'You feel sorry for *him?*' hissed back the Princess Kara.

All her life she had known she must marry Oslaf. All her life she had fought to bury that knowledge. Today she could hide from it no longer. This was Finnglas's doing.

The king was leaning towards her, his grey beard quivering with anger. His voice cracked like unsafe ice.

'Does my own daughter say *No* to Jarlath of the Wolves?'

The word was crying in her heart. But another voice she feared more was chanting mercilessly,

Your daughter bows to what we say.
She does not scorn your royal will.
She knows my wolves beneath the hill.
She would not dare to disobey.'

The bones of her fingers locked together. Her fair head bowed, that had always been carried so haughtily. Her lids lowered over her fierce grey eyes. The whole hall waited.

'Well . . . daughter? Have you nothing to say to me?'

'Yes,' whispered Kara, very low.

'Louder. I cannot hear you.'

'Yes,' murmured Kara, lifting her tear-bright eyes to him.

'Louder still. Before all my court. You will wed Oslaf, prince of Bergenring?'

'Yes!' she cried out of the bitterness of her heart, tossing back the golden braids as she raised her proud head.

'Yes. I will marry him!'

What else could she say?

Far to the south her father's ship sped over the sea, carrying Finnglas to freedom. The sailor-princess leaned out over the prow, straining for a sight of the islands of Britain, while Arthmael raced their bow-wave. Behind her, a red-haired fisher-boy guided the helm, casting a longing look back at Senargad. On, on they flew, to the first grey glimpse of land and the sound of mermaid's singing.

4

Larsa, the potter's daughter, walked the beach between the forest and the sea's edge. The kiln was always hungry for wood to fire the blue-black jars and bowls. Too early yet for the winter storms to tear dead branches from the living trees. The sap was still high. But the breeze blew suddenly cold across her bare arms and legs. It came from the north. The year had begun to turn.

If there was fuel to be found today it might come not from the forest but from the sea. Last night's storm should have carried fresh driftwood to the tide-line and beached it on the sand.

She stood rubbing her brown, muscled arms to warm them and screwed up her eyes against the sun. The waves ran high in the sound this morning, glittering blue after the rain. Roofs shone gold from the summer's thatching. A dearer gold gleamed on the king's palace roof across the water. Something dark bobbed between the waves. A porpoise? There was another. And another. The waves washed them almost to her feet.

They were not living, leaping creatures. But they were what she was looking for. Stout planks of wood. She paddled into the surf and seized one. It was not yet heavy with water. The end was sharply splintered, the fresh, pale wood newly exposed to the sun. More were floating in on every wave. Larsa ran here and there, splashing, as she tried to gather it all before the current swept it past her. There was more than she could hold.

She straightened up and put her fingers to her lips. She blew a shrilling whistle through them, sharp as a sea-bird. Three corn-bright heads popped out of the tall grass beside the homestead. Three little figures came racing along the sand, her small sister Hygd in a pale green dress the colour of dry moss, and her younger brothers, Bor and Sigi in tunics of russet and yellow. They saw the timber in her arms and knew at once that she needed help.

'Race you!'

'Bet I can get more than you can.'

Bor and Sigi dashed waist-deep into the swift-running waves. But little Hygd worked faster still. She snatched at planks that floated in to the shallows and dragged them up beyond the reach of the sea before running back for more.

The boys and Larsa waded ashore, dragging their dripping haul. They heaped them on Hygd's little pile. Soon it began to look like the midwinter bonfire.

Bor trailed a longer stave up the beach and dropped it with the rest.

'You know,' he said, 'there's something funny about these planks. They're not straight.'

Larsa, Sigi and Hygd looked at their hoard. He was right. These were not the raw, unformed lengths of a deck cargo. Each piece was cunningly curved, shaped to a particular place and purpose, the edges planed to fit against each other.

'You're right,' said Sigi. 'These are ship's timbers.'

Larsa felt she had known it when she first saw the dark flotsam. But she had not wanted to believe it. She had preferred to shut her mind and think only of cheerful things. Of firewood, furnaces and baking pottery. Not of wet, cold death.

Now they stood at the water's edge with the wind tugging at their skirts.

'Poor souls,' said Larsa softly.

There was much wreckage still, floating on past the headland.

'Come on,' said Sigi. 'We're losing half of it.'

He waded out again.

'Be careful of the current,' Larsa called.

Next moment there was a cry from him. It was not a shout of alarm but of discovery. Bor splashed to help him.

Together they brought ashore a stem of timber, square-cut, massively carved at one end. A grey wolf's head, with scarlet tongue. One ear and eye had been torn away.

'Look at this, Larsa!'

The salt wind had made Larsa's lips stiff and dry. She licked them nervously as she stared at the unmistakable figurehead. One gold-painted eye glared back at her evilly.

'These were the king's wolf-ships!'

The three younger children gasped.

'Smashed?' said Sigi wonderingly.

'Was there a big battle?' asked Hygd.

'I bet King Jarlath's very angry.' Bor's chuckle sounded scared.

All four of them gazed across the sound, at the glittering roofs of the palace of Senargad. What was happening there?

'I don't think we should burn it,' said Larsa, looking down again at the broken figurehead. 'We ought to tell somebody.'

'Look,' said Hygd, catching her arm. 'There's something else coming.'

Softer shapes were drifting past them, lapped by the early morning waves. The sodden carcases of wolves and galley-slaves.

They stood in silence. The boys did not want to enter the water now. The wreckage hung on the tossing swell, pulled in by the tide, pushed out by the wind. They let it go.

'Run!' said Larsa, taking control again. 'Tell Father and Mother what we've found. They'll know what to do.'

Bor and Sigi raced back across the sand towards the low thatched house. Both wanted to be first to tell the news. Larsa began to walk along the headland. Hygd followed her. As they rounded the point, the wind fell still, screened by the birchwood. A wide bay stretched south, its waters calm and green. Here more flotsam had come to rest along the tideline in a dark ring.

Larsa walked on slowly, scuffing through shells. Then she stopped and looked down. A little gasp broke from her. The broken wood at her feet was painted too. But not

21

with the war-wolves of King Jarlath. There was a tumbling pattern of green, like gaily-tossing waves or seaweed. And leaping through it, dark blue and white, the figure of a laughing dolphin.

A name came soundlessly to Larsa's lips.

Hygd caught up with her and saw it too. She slipped her small cold hand into her sister's and looked up into Larsa's eyes.

'It's Erc's boat, isn't it?'

5

The girls turned back to the bay with sinking hearts. They started to hurry along the shore. Here and there a bundled body lay at the water's edge; ship-slave, warrior-wolf. There was no life in any of them. They were not many. Not one of them was a red-haired fisher-boy. The girls tugged them gently out of the reach of the rocking waves. Larsa straightened up, relief in her face.

'He's not here.'

The wreckage was thinning out, the wind carrying it further south. Larsa and Hygd walked back towards the point.

'What's happened to Erc?' Hygd asked. 'Is he drowned? Was he in a fight?'

'I don't know. There is something strange. But let's not give up hope. There weren't many bodies, were there? I think most of them must have been saved.'

They had almost reached the headland when they heard the shouts of men's voices from the other side. Larsa gave a sudden gasp. She ran forward to where the tell-tale wreckage of the dolphin-painted boat still strewed the sand. Swiftly she scooped it up in her strong arms. Hygd asked no questions but did the same, her little legs running up and down the tide-line like an oyster-catcher. She ploughed after Larsa up the sand into the shelter of the wood.

Larsa was already digging a hollow in the boggy ground between the birch trees. She dropped the timbers of Erc's boat into it. Hygd added hers. Black water oozed over it. Larsa kicked back the broken peat and smoothed it over. She wiped her muddy hands on her blue dress and smiled at Hygd, putting her finger to her lips.

'There! Let's keep it a secret, shall we?'

Hand in hand they strolled back through the trees to the side of the headland facing Senargad.

There was great excitement on the beach. A crowd of men and women had gathered round the wreckage, with other children. Their father, Witgan, was there, with several more farmers, speckled with gold dust from threshing corn. Their mother, Gerda, her arms smeared with potter's clay. The smith, his face streaked black with charcoal. Bor and Sigi were telling excitedly how they had found it.

Their father seized the splintered wolf's head and brandished it high.

'I'm taking this to the palace. It's likely King Jarlath will give a reward for information like this.'

The smith chuckled. 'More likely he'll say you stole it and clap you in prison.'

An angry mutter went round the crowd. But Witgan would not put down his trophy. He still clutched it greedily as they walked on past the point, as the girls had done. Larsa and Hygd followed silently.

As they saw the bay, Larsa hissed, 'Our footsteps!'

But they need not have worried. There was a cry of doubt and alarm as the crowd saw the beached bodies. They all rushed to look closer and then edged back. The sand was trampled by fifty feet. The people shook their heads in sorrow over the drowned slaves. No one wanted to touch the wolves. Some of the men and children went running back to the village and returned with carts pulled by sturdy ponies. They loaded them with everything they could find, even, reluctantly, the wolves. The Rhymester's magic warriors looked less frightening now, with the wet fur flattened against ribs and legs.

The beach lay clean and fresh as the carts trundled away, with Bor and Sigi riding triumphantly on the first one with their father. The sea was innocently empty. Larsa and Hygd smiled knowingly at each other.

'Hurry up,' called their mother. 'King's gold or not, there's the kiln to be fired, and pots to be made and the dinner to cook.'

Now wood must be gathered all over again. The girls searched the fringes of the forest, scuffling in the sand for buried branches.

'Lovely morning.'

They both spun round as if they had been caught doing something guilty. Larsa could not resist a quick backward glance to where they had buried Erc's painted prow between the trees. But Hygd was staring in bewilderment at the empty beach.

'Makes you feel good to be alive, doesn't it?'

The strange voice seemed to come from nowhere.

Larsa walked down to the water's edge to see further round the headland. Nothing moved except the dancing waves.

'Smile!' The whistling call was so near it made her jump. 'The sun is shining.'

'Look!' shouted Hygd, pointing into the water. 'There he is!'

He was surfing in on the crest of a combing breaker. He dived through the green wall and disappeared. Next moment he came floating into the shallows almost to their feet. But before the sand could hold him he whisked his powerful tail and shot out into the cool depths again.

'It's a dolphin!' cried Larsa.

He was the living reality of the leaping image Erc had painted on his boat. More alive than anyone could imagine. Springing into the sun. Diving to the sea-bed. Dancing as though the sea had just been recreated.

Larsa waded into the waves to meet him.

'I know who you are,' she called as he flashed past her, foam glittering on his scarred black sides. 'Erc told me. You're Lok the Lucky, aren't you?'

He swam out to sea, eyes twinkling as he whistled back to her.

'In the south they call me Arthmael, the Clown, the Dancer. By any name, in any land, I am this world's Fool.'

He ran in again, his face bright with silent laughter.

'That is why I was, and shall be, a prince.'

25

He was gone again, but not for long.

'I think you're lovely.' Hygd stroked his head as he surfaced, hovering, in front of her.

'So are you, Hygd,' Arthmael said tenderly. 'So are you. Lovely and lovable.'

Then he rose straight up on his great tail and shouted to the dazzling sky.

'So is this day! So is this world! So is everyone!'

He crashed down into the waves in an explosion of spray. Larsa staggered back, wet to the shoulders now. Arthmael rolled over on his side, one small eye watching her.

'Isn't that true, Larsa?'

She rubbed her arms and shivered in the cold breeze.

'No, it's not. You can't mean that. Don't you know what happened here today? There must have been a battle. So many wrecked ships, drowned slaves, dead wolves. And Erc . . . '

Was that a tear, like a jewel in the corner of his eye?

'Yet you have been happy other mornings, haven't you? You thought the world was beautiful.'

'Yes, of course,' she admitted.

'Were there no wars then? No deaths? No shipwrecks?'

'Not here.'

'They were real, though you did not think of them. Yet so was the sun. It is still real this morning. Go on, you can feel it warming your skin, can't you? And the sand? Take up a handful. A thousand tiny shells in the hollow of your palm. Lift your eyes to the sea. Purple on the rocks, green over sand, brighter than any opal. Isn't this all wonderful? Doesn't it make you rejoice?'

'Not today.'

'Especially today. Look at it well, Larsa. Love it. Hold on to its beauty. This day is all you have.'

He soared into the sun, did a double somersault, dived into the green waves and vanished completely.

6

Larsa and her mother squatted against the sunny south wall. Their fists and arms were dark with wetted clay, their faces smeared with drying streaks of paler grey. Their strong, clever hands pounded it like dough, hollowed it, turned and shaped it. The pots rose between their coaxing fingers, shapely, strong, serviceable, like their makers. From time to time they pushed back the falling hair from their sweating brows. Then they damped the surface of the bowl, smoothed it, pressed it with knuckles, straw, shells, a scratching nail. Patterns wove around the rim with practised speed.

Hygd fetched water for them, fed the fire already roaring beneath the kiln, and played with scraps of clay. She shaped doll-size pots with tiny fingers that were already learning their trade.

'Funny,' said Larsa, tearing off a wodge of clay and slapping it down on the board in front of her. 'This morning I thought the year had turned. And yet sitting here out of the wind, you could believe it was still the middle of summer.'

Hygd jumped to her feet. 'The carts are coming back from Senargad! I can see ours in front!'

Their mother, Gerda, shaded her eyes. 'At least the king's not put your father in prison.'

The carts were filing over the bridge. The ponies were running at a fast gait between a trot and a gallop, as though the men were in a hurry to bring news. But the carts were heavy and the pace still too slow for Bor and Sigi. They leaped down and came running towards the house, shouting.

'The king's prisoners have escaped!'

'There was the Princess Finnglas, an Irish monk and a cat.'

27

'They say it was the white cat set them free, but someone must have helped him.'

'The king's wild with rage. They stole his magic ship.'

'The Rhymester spoke the spell and raised the Wolf-Guard.'

'They went tearing after them. But then the Dolphin came.'

'He called a hundred whales!'

'That's how the fleet was wrecked.'

'They landed the wolves and the galley-slaves miles from Senargad.'

Larsa's hand was at her throat. 'What of the prisoners . . . and the one who helped them?'

'They got clean away.'

'And the king was going to marry that princess. He'd ordered a great feast. So now the Princess Kara's got to get married instead.'

The cart came swaying up the track and creaked to a halt. The pony, Bilberry, hung his sweating head.

Gerda said to her husband, 'I can see from your face the king didn't give you a fortune for your trouble.'

Witgan glared at her. 'Not he! Bad news travels fast. He knew half of it already.'

He stamped into the house, leaving the boys to unyoke Bilberry. He said to his wife and elder daughter as they followed him, 'But there is gold to be had. There was a traitor in the city. He fled with the prisoners. The king has sworn a chest of gold to the first one who names him.'

He did not see his little daughter, Hygd, listening round-eyed in the doorway.

Gerda fetched bread and herring for their father, and then the children ate.

Witgan tore at a crust. 'How I would love to put my finger on the one who did it. Who helped the cat to let those prisoners loose. Just think what we could do with a chest of gold, wife!'

'Naming's one thing. Catching's another,' Gerda said sensibly. 'I thought you said they'd got clean away.'

28

'But there's *ten* chests of gold for the one who brings him back!' exclaimed Bor.

Larsa had been eating steadily with her eyes cast down, as if nothing was wrong. Now her hand trembled.

But Sigi cried, 'They say the Rhymester's going mad because . . . '

'Hush!' snapped Gerda. 'Best not speak that name in this house. It's unlucky to hear it.'

'All right, then,' said Sigi. 'The *king's* going mad. It's the same thing, isn't it? They say he never does anything without *him*. He's wild because the Dolphin beat him. They say he won't raise wolves next time, it'll be something worse that he's got in his power.'

'Sea-serpents!'

'Giant crows!'

'Trolls!'

'They won't catch him!'

A small, sure voice came from the other side of the table. Hygd was looking at Larsa, with that same happy, knowing smile in her little blue eyes. Larsa shook her head slightly and frowned a warning. But it was too late. Bor had seen that look. He understood.

His stool scraped back. He jumped up, red with excitement. His finger pointed at Hygd.

'She knows! She knows who did it, don't you, Hygd?'

Hygd's hand flew to her mouth.

Witgan was on his feet too.

'Then tell us, girl! Why, in the name of Thor, didn't you open your mouth sooner? Sigi! Run and saddle Bilberry as fast as you can! I'll gallop back to the palace if I have to whip the hide off him. Now, girl, the name! The name!'

Two huge tears brimmed in Hygd's blue eyes.

Her father seized her arm. 'Quick, girl, out with it! Do you want somebody else to get there first and claim the gold?'

The tears rolled silently down her cheeks.

'Right! If that's the way of it, I'll make you talk.' His face was black with anger. He tore the belt from his tunic and

29

swung the leather strap aloft. The other hand grasped Hygd, who gave a frightened moan.

But before the belt could come lashing down across Hygd's back, Larsa had moved. Her strong hands gripped her father's wrist and forced it back.

'Don't you dare!' she panted. 'Please, father, don't touch her!'

Witgan whirled round, letting go of Hygd. Astonishment and rage battled in his eyes.

'What did you say? Do *both* my daughters defy me? By the demon Mimir who stole Odin's eye, I'll be master in this house!'

Larsa planted her hands on her hips and strove to look at him steadily.

'Then beat me, if you must. I know everything Hygd knows. Thrash it out of me, if you can. *Run*, Hygd.'

The little girl bolted out of the door.

There was a moment's silence. Gerda gasped and twisted her apron between her hands. Then Bor shouted, 'I'll get her!' and tore after Hygd.

For a moment tall Sigi stood undecided, his frightened eyes darting between his running brother and his furious father. Then he took to his heels and raced after Bor.

Hygd flew out of the house. Golden-Spring, the cow, gave a bellow of fright and galloped up the meadow. Big Bor was gaining on his sister. With a sob she doubled back around the house. When the boys rushed round the corner and faced the sea, there was no sign of her.

Inside the barn at the end of the house, Bilberry stamped and whinnied. Bor darted in through the other door. Straw-dust was whirling in a shaft of sunshine. The hem of Hygd's green dress whisked into the little hay-loft in the rafters. Bor gave a crow of triumph and pounded up the ladder, with Sigi close on his heels.

Hygd cowered, trapped, against a bale of straw. Bor flung himself on her.

'Got you! Now you're going to tell us! Who was it?'

'No! No!' sobbed Hygd.

30

He twisted her arm.

'Tell me. We want that gold.'

'No! No! No!'

Sigi grabbed him from behind.

'Leave her alone! Who cares about the king's gold? Don't you hit her!'

The two boys fought in the straw. Bor was older and heavier, but Sigi was taller. His long arms thrashed and wrapped themselves round Bor's body. But the older boy broke free with a blow to the chin that sent Sigi spinning across the loft.

He pounced on Hygd and forced her arm behind her back.

'Now, are you going to tell?'

Her arm was bent almost to breaking point.

'It was Erc!' she wept. 'Young Erc, that was Big Erc's son.'

Erc, the red-haired fisherman's son. Erc, whose father had been lost overboard in a storm. Erc, whose mother the king had sold to the south as a slave. They knew him too well. He had let them fish with him on summer evenings. He had taught them to row, to swim, to tie curious knots with rope.

Sigi rose like a pale ghost in the corner of the loft.

'You won't tell on him, will you Bor? If you do, Father will sell him to the king.'

From the living-room below they heard their father's angry shout. There was a cry from Larsa, then a ringing crash.

Bor hesitated. His mouth started to form words, but left them unspoken.

He muttered, 'They won't catch him, anyway. It's only the name. We'd have *one* chest of gold.'

'But what if the Rhymester . . . '

Hygd clapped her hand to her lips, as though to catch back the unlucky name.

'They'll be miles away. Even his magic couldn't reach them now. With the wind behind them, they could be home in Ireland before winter.'

'But Erc? What if he comes back?'

'He wouldn't dare.'

'Bor!' pleaded Sigi.

'Get off. Let me think.'

He started to climb down the ladder.

Sigi and Hygd looked at each other with scared eyes. Hygd's face was tear-stained, woeful.

'I told him because he was hurting me. I couldn't help it.

32

Even if Bor keeps it secret, it won't be any good. If Father beats me, he'll make me tell him too.'

Bor crossed the barn. Bilberry nuzzled against his arm, but Bor pushed him away. He walked on to the living-room.

Their mother, Gerda, was backed into a corner, looking frightened. Larsa lay on the floor. A great black bruise was swelling on her forehead. One tooth was missing, and her lip was split. Witgan stood looking down at her, with his fists clenched at his sides.

Bor stopped, shocked. Thoughts of Erc, of gold, flew out of his head. He could only stare at his sister. Strong, laughing Larsa, lying on the floor among the broken bowls, with her eyes closed. He felt sick. He turned on his heel and walked swiftly out of the house. No one had noticed him.

It was a brilliant afternoon. The grass was vivid green in the meadow, and the cow tore at it with black, velvety lips. The stubble-fields shone gold. The pale green leaves of birch trees made the shadows dance. Over them all stretched the vault of the sky, so intensely blue it hurt his eyes to look at it.

He could hardly see where he was going. He stumbled on towards the beach. He collapsed on a rock and sat for a long time with his face in his hands, hiding his eyes from the dazzle of the water.

A plop, like a large fish rising. From habit, Bor raised his head to look.

A blunt-nosed dolphin. Dark above, silvery beneath, with a golden stripe down his side cut with jagged scars.

Bor stared at him. He had never seen a dolphin so close. The dolphin did nothing. He hung in front of Bor, with the waves washing over him, and his keen, intelligent eyes gazing back into Bor's.

Bor began to feel uncomfortable. He picked up a fistful of sand and started to trickle it from one hand to the other. It escaped through his fingers till his hands were empty. He looked up again. The dolphin's gaze had not moved.

'What do you want? Who are you?' he asked, half cross and half afraid.

A smile flashed across the dolphin's face like sunshine. 'Oh, good! I wondered when you'd notice me.' And then his look was still and stern again.

'Notice you! How can I help noticing you, when you won't stop staring at me? Who are you?'

There was no answer. Bor got up. He started to walk up and down the sand. He wanted to run away, but it seemed silly.

He faced the sea again.

'I'm not afraid of you!' He tried to shout it, but his voice cracked. He knew it wasn't true.

Still Arthmael watched him.

'What do you *want?*' cried the boy.

'What do *you* want, Bor? What are you going to do?'

'I don't know, do I? Go away and let me think!'

'I would rather stay and help you think. But you can go. I can't stop you, can I? A dolphin has no hands, you see. I can't make you stay with me, if you don't want to.'

For a wonderful moment, Bor realized it was true. All he had to do was walk up the beach. And the dolphin had no feet. It couldn't follow him. He could just go home. Then he remembered his father's clenched fists, Larsa's bruised mouth, Hygd's tearful eyes in front of his and Sigi's pale, shocked face. He needed help to face them.

He turned back angrily.

'What difference would it make? Erc's escaped, hasn't he? He hasn't got any family left here. Who would I be betraying if I told on him?'

Arthmael looked at him sadly.

'Bor.'

'Yes?'

'Oh, Bor! That was not a question, but the answer.'

Arthmael rolled his great head backward, smiled up at the sun, and with a flick of his tail, dived beneath the glittering waves.

Bor waited. He did not know if he wanted the dolphin to reappear or not. At last he realized that Arthmael had gone. He was alone with himself. He did not like the thought.

34

He started to walk rapidly back to the house. In spite of the sunshine, the wind seemed to blow more coldly. Witgan met him in the doorway. His eyes were hungry. In the room behind him Larsa was sitting on a bench and Gerda was washing the blood from her face.

'Well? What have you got to tell me? Where is that brat, Hygd? I'll squeeze it out of her before the day is over.'

Bor still could not make up his mind what to do. His tongue seemed trapped in his mouth. He walked past his father without speaking and climbed the ladder.

The loft was empty. There was only Bilberry in the barn, and the cow and the poultry in the meadow. Hygd and Sigi had gone.

8

'I will not tell you.'

For the second time in two days the Princess Kara heard a girl defy the king, her father. And such a common girl. Not even a foreign princess this time. A big, brown, red-cheeked girl, with shoulder-muscles as big as turnips. A pot-woman's daughter. Her fat, flaxen plaits were dirtied with clay and you could see from her blue dress where she had wiped her hands on her hips. The skirt of it was stained with a salt tide-mark, as though she had been paddling in the sea. And her face! Kara looked away in disgust. The swelling over one eye, the cut lip, that black gap where a tooth was missing. She would be marked for life, whatever punishment they gave her.

The thanes stood round the hall to add their voices to the king's judgment. There were no women present but Kara and her maid-servants, behind the high table on the dais. The hall was guarded by men again. The Rhymester's wolves had returned with their sodden tails between their legs. Now they were once more human warriors in grey, hairy cloaks. They had a surly, hang-dog look.

'She knows, your Majesty!' Witgan shouted. 'That's why I brought her to you. She doesn't deny she knows the traitor's name. I couldn't beat it out of her but you will have better luck. She cannot refuse to tell King Jarlath of the Wolves. Yet remember, sire, it was I, Witgan of Thorkelsdal, who brought you the secret you wanted. Look, here she is.'

The king rose slowly, the gold edge of his cloak unfolding like serpent-coils. His voice was gravel-sharp.

'What age is this we live in, when daughters defy their fathers, when women argue with men, when serfs refuse to obey their lawful king?'

'But not for long,' hissed a soft voice behind him.
'She is afraid.
We'll change her song,
This lawless maid.'

He was right. Larsa was afraid. A pulse throbbed in her throat. Her blue eyes went round the hall searching for help. They came to the only women there. But the Princess Kara looked away. So did most of her waiting-women. Only one pair of eyes stared back at Larsa in silent sympathy. A round, soft, sorrowful face. But what could Elli do? She was only Kara's maid.

The king turned to the Rhymester with a thin smile.

'How do you suggest we make her sing? With whips? Shall we roast her on a stake over a fire? Or have you other ideas?'

'Sire! I've beaten her already. You can see for yourself,' Witgan gulped. 'And it didn't work. She's very stubborn. But the fire! What if she still doesn't talk? What if she dies?'

'And the secret dies with her? And you lose your hope of gold.' The king's smile was turned evilly upon Witgan. 'A strange hope, that. You cannot prise the name from her, and so you came to me to force it out of her. And still you hope for my reward?'

'Not . . . not a *whole* chest of gold, sire,' choked Witgan. 'I thought . . . half?'

It was Larsa's turn to meet the iron-grey eyes.

'You see what you have cost your father already? Half a chest of gold. Think what that could have bought your parents. You have a mother, haven't you? Think of her growing old. Sick. Husbandless. You have brothers and sisters? What of them? What if you cost them not just half a chest of gold? What if they lost their home, their farm, their animals, everything? Imagine your little family begging in the snow.'

Witgan had turned white. This wasn't going as he had planned.

Jarlath's voice was gentle now, like water trickling

under ice.

'The name. One small, short name. He's gone, you know. He and those Irish thieves have stolen over the horizon in my gold, wolf-prowed ship. What harm can you do him now? Just say his name.'

She would not listen. She must shut her ears to that coaxing, terrifying voice. She must shut her eyes to the pictures he was trying to hold before her. Surely he couldn't mean it. Her mother? Her brothers? Hygd? She must not imagine it. She must think of something else.

The flash of gulls' wings soaring above the sea on the wind. The bursts of spray as the waves smacked against the rocks. A handful of sand. A thousand tiny, coloured shells. The shade of silver-stemmed birch trees dappling the grass, and the deep blue sky dancing between the tossing leaves.

A strange voice saying, '*Hold on to its beauty.*'

That other voice was speaking now. She tried to keep her mind's defences firm against it. But it was too powerful for her. The Rhymester's rhythms battered at her brain. The cold tide of his words swept in and engulfed her heart.

'Two days till Kara's wedding-morn.
Till then imprisoned let her wait
In serpent-circled dark forlorn,
Then speak that name or face her fate.'

Standing with her back to the door, Larsa was the last to understand. She saw the Rhymester's talon reach out from his cloak and beckon, summoning. Not to her, but to the doorway behind her. She had been terrified that he would raise the Wolf-Guard, but now she saw that they were terrified themselves. Several of the women looked about to faint, and the princess was pale and staring.

She heard a shuffle over the stones, felt the palace creak and shake as something squeezed between the doorposts. Sliding now over the floorboards with a soft hiss. Her father was backing away. Brave warriors were flattening themselves against the walls. The king was smiling, beckoning like the

38

Rhymester, coaxing. A foul smell reached her nostrils.

Something was flowing round her. Dark green, flecked with arrowheads of black that swelled and shrank as it poured its body past her. Slippery, shiny scales, sharp-edged as knives. Short stumps of legs that could not hold the dragging belly from the floor. A weaving, worm-like head with sightless eyes, scenting its way in coils around her.

She watched it in petrified horror. Erc's name was crying in her heart. But still she would not speak. The Serpent of Senargad wound itself three times about her, squeezing closer with each coil.

The blunt, blind snout searched for the door and slithered towards it. Two hind legs scrabbled the floor, dragging the scaly, pointed tail through the dust. It left a glistening, golden trail behind it.

The Princess Kara stared after Larsa. Only her bare, clay-marked feet could be seen, two dangling arms, a fallen, flaxen head.

Poor fool, to think she could defy them! Yet there had been something astonishing about this pot-girl. For a few moments, while Witgan raged, and King Jarlath threatened and the Wolf-Guard fingered their spears, there had been a strange light in her face. She had looked almost . . . *happy*.

Outside there was utter silence in the city. The people of Senargad cowered behind closed shutters. Even the birds stopped singing while the Worm of Senargad passed.

9

Bor kicked a stone through the dust. It was a long trudge on foot to Senargad. He was not sure why he was going, or what he was going to do when he got to the palace. Behind him, his mother was crying in the kitchen, Golden-Spring was lowing mournfully to be milked, and the empty kiln was already growing cold. Sigi and Hygd had not come home.

Bor had not dared to ask his father if he could ride in the cart, jolting towards the city for the second time that terrible day. He did not want to sit opposite Larsa, obstinate, disobedient, now her father's prisoner. Would she guess that he too knew the traitor's name? And what should he do, now that he held the secret?

A chest full of gold.

He crossed the bridge and the palace rose clearly in front of him, gilded wolf-heads rearing on every gable-end. The smaller, jostling roofs of the town's houses covered the rest of the hill on which it stood. Outside the walls, near the water's edge, were scattered the humble cottages of fisher-folk. Bor found his feet drawn unwillingly off the road towards one of these.

It leaned for shelter against the side of a massive boulder. It was hardly bigger than an upturned boat. The hanging thatch was patched with moss. The window was shuttered.

Bor lifted the shutter aside and peered in. There was not much to see. The hearth was dead. The room was empty. Outside there was none of the litter of everyday life. Everything had been tidied away.

A woman was gathering up her washing from the rocks nearby. Bor called to her.

'Have you seen Erc lately? Do you know where he is?'

'He's not been home for weeks. Since his father died and his mother was sold, poor soul, young Erc's spent most of the summer in his fishing-boat. I don't expect we'll see him again till they lay the boats up.'

He watched her face. She glanced at the palace when she spoke of Erc's mother, but only for a moment. She hadn't guessed.

Bor put the shutter back and walked on to the harbour. Some of the boats were already tied up at the staithe. Other spaces were empty. In a few weeks' time all the craft would be pulled up on the shore, out of reach of the winter's storms.

Erc's boat was missing.

He sauntered along the quay, trying to keep his voice casual.

'Have you seen Erc? Young Erc, that was Big Erc's son?'

One of the fishermen shrugged.

'Not today. His boat was here last night. But he was gone early this morning. Nothing odd about that. He's often away for days at a time. He ties up in a fiord or on one of the islands at night. He's no love for this city since the wolves took his mother. He'll come back when he's fish to sell.'

They went on checking their nets. No one was worried. It was nothing unusual that Erc was missing. But what would they do if they knew how much his name was worth?

He stood there watching, almost willing the thought into their minds. Surely they had heard about the reward for the traitor who had helped the monk and the cat and the Princess Finnglas to escape? But they knew him too well. It was only Erc, the red-haired orphan boy. Nobody important. How could he have threatened the king and the Rhymester and the terrible wolves?

He went on through the guarded gates into the town. His father and Larsa would be at the palace by now. Perhaps — the thought came to him suddenly like a flash of sunshine — perhaps Larsa had given way. Perhaps she had already told the king everything. It would all be over. She would be free. Their father would have the chest of gold.

Bor could go home and nobody need ever know he had shared her secret.

He was climbing the hill, pushing through crowds up the cobbled street, in sight of the grey-cloaked sentries now. The sun sank lower over the sea behind him. The air began to hiss. A voice chanted as though the palace itself was speaking. It was throbbing from every stone in the city.

> ' . . . *Till then imprisoned let her wait*
> *In serpent-circled dark forlorn,*
> *Then speak that name, or face her fate.*'

It was as if a curfew-bell had tolled. The street emptied instantly. Shutters were slammed, doors bolted. In moments everyone was hidden inside the houses.

Bor was left alone in the street where the very air quivered with an approaching menace. He bolted round a corner and hid himself behind a pile of rubbish.

There was a scraping, sliding, sucking sound coming slowly closer. The walls of the house he crouched behind began to tremble. Then a taint of corruption fouled the air, like the stench of rotting flesh. The sunlight dimmed and a dog howled from inside the house. Shivers of horror ran through Bor. Long, long the Serpent seemed to take in passing.

Bor had buried his face against his knees. He did not want to look. He guessed too horribly what he would see. But at last he crept back to the corner of the street.

Gold. Glittering, mocking gold in a trail that led from the palace steps. The slime ended at the city gate. Something dark, huge and unlovely was heaving its way through that opening, making the iron clank hollowly. He had a forlorn glimpse of a fair head, two clay-daubed feet. The Worm was carrying Larsa in its coils. She had not betrayed Erc. Outside the city the Worm swung its head, scenting. It turned for the mountains, going north in the red glare of sunset.

The boy's feet moved him miserably towards the palace. He did not want to be alone. He needed his father's familiar face. There were no sentries now guarding the golden portals, nor on the steps, nor at the palace door. Bor walked carefully, avoiding the slimy, golden trail.

He tiptoed up to the hall. The first thing he heard was his father's voice, gabbling wildly.

'I have another, younger daughter. She knows the secret too. She ran away. But you could track her. You could find where she is hiding, couldn't you? She's only small. You'd have it out of her in no time.'

He spoke to the gold-clad king, but a shadow slid out from behind Jarlath. The grey-cloaked Rhymester glided across the hall and whispered in the ears of three warriors.

Pink human tongues licked dry men's lips. In nervousness? Anticipation?

'*Harbard. Thorvild. Ref.*'

There was a gust of movement, like a sudden eddy of mist. And then there were three huge wolves, running red tongues over coal-black gums.

> '*From harbouring home or woodland wild*
> *Track down and seize the treacherous child.*'

Bor cringed back against the corner as the wolves sped past him.

As soon as they were out of sight, he turned and ran. He didn't care who saw him now. It didn't matter what they thought. Away from the palace, out of the city, past the harbour, to the lonely, wave-wet beach.

He sat hunched on a rock in the chilly evening wind, listening to the sigh of the sea. He was staring intently at the waves, and trying to pretend to himself that he wasn't. He longed for the dolphin to come back. He wanted someone to tell him what to do. But he was afraid of what it might be.

He had only to go back to the palace. He could say one short name. He would save Larsa from the Worm and Hygd and Sigi from the wolves. Or he could do as they had done. He could side with Erc against the king. He could draw the Rhymester's anger on to himself.

He sat for a long time while the evening darkened. Arthmael did not appear. Bor went slowly home. He still said nothing.

10

'Come on, can't you?' Fear made Sigi's voice sharp and angry.

'Where are we going?' wailed Hygd, tripping over brambles for the twentieth time.

'I don't know. We've just got to get away. We've got to find somebody to help us.'

'What did Father *do* to Larsa?'

'I don't know,' said Sigi again.

They had run as far as they could. Up the meadow, into the trees, along the paths of the woodcutters. At last they had stumbled to a walk, with the breath rasping in their chests and a stitch stabbing their sides. Still they hurried on panting, up threads of paths that were hardly more than deer-tracks now. The slender birches had given way to bigger, older trees. Now even the brambles were thinning out. There were soft brown leaves underfoot, wide spaces between the giant tree-trunks. Mist drifted under the branches like grey hair.

'I want to go home,' wavered Hygd.

'We can't,' said Sigi.

'How much further is it?'

'How do I know, if I don't know where we're going? But there must be another side to the forest, mustn't there? There'll be people there. Perhaps they won't have heard about the Princess Finnglas. They won't know about the reward and Erc's boat. They'll look after us. They'll let us stay there till it's all over.'

'Sigi?' asked Hygd, when they had walked some way without speaking. 'How will we know when it's over?'

Under the towering oaks and the dark-boughed fir trees

45

the sunlight hardly penetrated. Darkness fell much sooner here than in sea-bright Senargad. There were no cows lowing at milking-time, no sleepy gossip of hens, no stamp of a horse in the stable. Only the deep and ancient silence of the forest.

'I'm frightened,' said Hygd. 'Will there be wolves?'

Sigi put his arm round her shoulders. He was afraid too.

'There might be,' he said. 'But they'd only be ordinary wolves. Not magic ones.'

'Will they eat us?'

'I don't see why they should. Not unless they were very hungry. After all, they're only big dogs, aren't they?'

'I'm afraid of big dogs.'

The darkness was deepening, and still there was no sign of the forest's end.

'Sigi?'

'Yes.'

'Will there be bears?'

'Oh, shut up, can't you? I don't know everything, do I?'

They were tired and hungry, but they walked till they could walk no longer. Their eyes were closing. At last the mist turned to a gentle, pattering rain that gathered on the leaves and dripped on their heads. They found a hollow in the giant trunk of an oak and crept into its crumbling, fungus-fringed cave.

There were wolves. They growled warily at the rank scent of humans and trotted past the oak-tree, avoiding it. A bear ambled by. She sniffed at the hollow trunk for grubs, then found a fallen log. She rolled it over and scratched the rotting wood. For a long time she sat beside the oak-tree, scooping maggots into her mouth with her big curved claws. Then she blundered on through the freshly-scented rain.

The rain fell, gently, insistently, washing the forest floor. The smell of Sigi and Hygd's footsteps trickled away into the bubbling brooks and disappeared in darkly-shadowed bogs. Three black-jowled wolves ran questing through the forest from the direction of Senargad. No woodland-dwellers this time. The rain beaded their coats and dripped from their noses. Their eyes glared red in the darkness. Their breath smoked with greed. But the forest had kept its secrets for thousands of years. Now it guarded two more.

Sigi and Hygd woke to the sound of running water and birdsong. All round them they could see nothing but trees.

'Which way do we go?' asked Hygd.

Sigi peered through the screen of branches to dazzling splinters of sun. He turned to his left.

'North,' he said. 'As far as we can from Senargad.'

About mid-morning the forest floor began to shelve downwards. The undergrowth was growing thicker, greener. There were handfuls of raspberries and fragrant mushrooms, not filling, but enough to blunt the pain in their empty bellies. As they began to see blue sky through the thinning treetops Hygd reached out for Sigi's hand.

They crossed a stream and they were in an open meadow. The dale was surrounded by hills. There was a farmstead, quite large and prosperous-looking. A scatter of smaller huts. Sheep starred the hills.

Sigi halted.

'This is the difficult bit. We've got to find friends. But how do we know if they *will* be friendly?'

'I'm hungry,' said Hygd.

They began to edge around the meadow, not wanting to walk out into the open. Hygd's pale green dress and Sigi's yellow tunic blended into the background of birch leaves. But long before they reached the nearest cottage they were seen.

The bright green grass bowed down like corn before the scythe. A speckled storm drove towards them, as if a feather pillow had burst in a gale. A terrible honking rose till it filled the valley and echoed back from the hills. Golden beaks were spear-tips at the end of outstretched necks. Grey wings beat thunderously in bone-breaking sweeps. From the leaders rushed a hiss as fierce as serpents.

Sigi tried to run and toppled backwards into the stream.

Hygd looked down at him crossly and then at the advancing storm.

'Don't be silly, Sigi. They're only geese.'

'I know! I'm afraid of geese,' gasped Sigi, coming up for air. 'Run, Hygd! Run!'

11

Hygd did not run. She stood, a small, green-clad figure, on the edge of the field. The geese swept round her like a blizzard, hooting and hissing. She was lost behind their whirling wings. Slowly the wing-beats lessened. Loose feathers drifted down through the air. Plump bodies settled over pink feet and gold bills were tucked into downy chins.

Hygd stayed quite still in the middle of their waddling circle, holding out small, open hands.

'Come on,' she coaxed. 'Nice chuckies.'

The honking died to a throaty gobble. They sounded embarrassed as they scolded each other.

'It's only a little girl.'

'Well, you can't be too careful these days.'

'We had to see.'

'Who started it, anyway?'

'Well, it's our meadow, isn't it? I didn't know she was harmless.'

'Look out, there's another of them.'

'Oh dear, oh my! Just look at him!'

'Tadpoles in his trousers!'

'Eels up his elbows!'

'Weed round his wings.'

'Arms, you fool. It's a human.'

'So it is.'

Sigi climbed dripping on to the bank.

'Oh, dear! I'm terribly sorry,' said a concerned voice.

A strange figure was standing behind the geese. She was hung with a collection of rags so faded and grubby you could hardly see that they had once been all the colours of the rainbow. Her thin face was scarred white by pox and her hair hung down over her shoulders in tangles. She was hardly older than Sigi.

But her mouth opened in a smile over perfect teeth and her violet eyes danced.

'You'd better take your clothes off and dry them in the sun,' she said to Sigi.

Hygd stood her ground and stared at the newcomer hopefully.

'Have you got anything to eat? . . . Please?'

The girl's face showed alarm. But she smiled again.

'Y-yes. Of course. How silly of me. I'll take you home. I'm Mai. I'm the goose-girl here,' she added unnecessarily.

'I'm Hygd, and this is Sigi,' said Hygd before her brother could stop her.

The geese were crooning now as they tore at the sweet cresses on the banks of the stream. Mai rounded them up with gentle taps of the birch twig she carried and drove them across the meadow in front of her. They complained as they waddled.

'Back and forth.'

'No peace for the wicked.'

'See them off.'

'Then give them dinner.'

'I don't know why we bother.'

Hygd trotted beside Mai. Sigi followed more slowly. He hadn't wanted Hygd to tell her their names. He had wanted them to be new people in an unknown place, until it was safe to reveal who they really were.

They were coming closer to the houses now. The farm had an unnaturally quiet air. No one was working out of doors. The horses were gone from the home-field.

'There's hardly anybody here but me,' said Mai. 'They've all ridden off to the king's wedding. News came that he was getting married to an Irish princess and my master was invited. So they loaded the horses with gifts and their finest clothes and off he rode with his family and half the servants. They'll be feasting in Senargad now.'

Sigi and Hygd looked at each other knowingly. Sigi put

his finger to his lips. This time Hygd gave no secrets away. Mai chattered on.

'The mistress was mad because she didn't have time to get a new dress for the wedding. That's a pity. She might have given the old one to the bailiff's wife. And *she* might have given one to the shepherd's wife. And perhaps she'd have given hers to the milkmaid. And the milkmaid might have given me her old skirt.'

Mai laughed and tightened the leather thong that held her rags together.

Sigi had been looking at the long thatched huts as they approached. The stout, plastered walls. The steeply-sloping roofs. But Mai ducked into a shelter so small and green he hadn't even noticed it.

The supple stems of alder saplings had been bent over and staked to the ground. Twigs had been woven crosswise in and out of them, and the whole had been covered over with turf. It was hardly bigger than a dog-kennel. Grass sprouted from it, and twenty kinds of wild flower blossomed on the roof.

Mai's earthy heels were still poking out of the doorway. There was no room to follow her. She wriggled out backwards, holding a chewed half-loaf of bread. She broke it in two and solemnly gave them each a piece.

'The blessing of my poor house upon you. Eat, and be welcome.'

Sigi's hand was half-way to his mouth when he paused. He saw Mai's thin, scarred face as she watched the bread about to disappear.

'This is all you've got, isn't it? We can't take it.'

Hygd's eyes brimmed with tears. She was very hungry. Mai's temper flared.

'I may be poor, but I'm not a beggar! It was mine to give if I wanted to, wasn't it?'

'But you'll share it with us, won't you? Go on, you must.' He broke off a smaller piece and handed it back to her. 'You ought to celebrate King Jarlath's wedding.'

He caught Hygd's eye. Hygd giggled and gave Mai a piece of bread too.

'Shall we tell her, Sigi? I think she's nice.'

They told her everything. How the king's bride, Finnglas, had run away to sea. How someone in Senargad had helped her escape. How the wolves had put out to sea after them. How whales had wrecked the fleet. How Erc's boat had come ashore, but with no body. Of Larsa and their father. Of how Bor knew the secret. And how Hygd had met the great dolphin, Arthmael.

'Do you think your brother Bor will tell what he knows?'

'I think he would have done if Father hadn't beaten Larsa. Now I'm not sure.'

'I wish I could see Arthmael,' sighed Mai. 'I'd love to have a friend like that. But I can't, can I? Not with a great forest between me and the sea.'

'I haven't met him either,' Sigi reminded her.

'The question is, what can I do to help you? My master Unferth is the king's friend. He'll be back as soon as they've married off Princess Kara. He'll know all about it.'

'He won't know about *us*, will he?' said Hygd, alarmed.

'Why not? You're important people. You're stopping King Jarlath getting what he wants.'

Hygd looked across at the houses nervously.

'Do you think anyone's seen us? Shouldn't we hide?'

'There's hardly anyone here. The shepherds are up on the summer pastures. Most of the others have gone to town. There's just the milkmaid and a few serfs and the children. But you're right. They mustn't know you're here until we've worked out what to tell them.'

She shooed them into the bothy, damp clothes and all, as if they were two of her geese. Hygd's face reappeared in the doorway.

'Mai! This is a present from me. Please take it.'

She was holding out the little green apron she had worn with her dress. Mai laughed with pleasure and tied it on over her rags. Then she sat in the sunshine, trying to think what to do. Her feathered flock grazed the grass around her, murmuring to her lovingly.

52

Mai did not have long to ponder. She saw the wolves a brief moment before the geese began to hiss.

12

The geese reared up, necks vertical, beaks honking at the sky. The three black wolves bounded the stream and raced through the grass towards them. Mai sprang up, too terrified to cry out, and seized her stick. Seeing her threatened, the geese spread their wings, flattened their necks, began to run towards the enemy, hissing and hooting terribly.

The wolves came on, eyes red, jaws grinning. The two sides, one grizzled black, one downy grey, met in the middle of the field in a storm of fur and feathers. Too late Mai shouted in protest and started to run to herd them off. But she was powerless to stop the battle.

It was brief and bloody. There could only be one end. Orange beaks speared into the wolves' muscled sides. Wings beat bruisingly about the snapping heads. In vain. Again and again the jaws crunched shut. Necks twisted and broke. Hot blood spouted over silky plumage. The grass was littered with feathered carcases.

Tears were pouring down Mai's face as her brave, foolish flock fought to save her from the wolves. She tried to beat them away with her birch twig, but they were deaf with defiance. The speckled wave of defenders was growing narrower. The eyes of the wolves sparkled hungrily as they fixed on the prey so nearly theirs. The girl-child.

Harbard, the leading wolf, plunged through the line, scattering the last of the screaming geese. Thorvild and Ref guarded his flanks, growling from wounded throats. They snuffled the scent of Hygd on Mai's hands, smelt Hygd's apron round her waist, and bayed in triumph. As their fangs closed imprisoningly on her arms Mai yelled to the blood-stained survivors, 'Fly!'

And over her shoulder to where Hygd and Sigi crouched horrified in the doorway.

'Fly! Fly!'

The wolves laughed without loosing their grip. What did they care where the mangled geese went? They were the Rhymester's creatures, doing the Rhymester's bidding, seizing the Rhymester's enemy. Bodies lay all around them. But the spell on the wolves was stronger than their hunger for flesh. They were starting to drag Mai with them towards the forest.

Still the geese would not yield and run. The old grey gander slashed at Harbard's rump. With a howl the wolf let go of Mai and sprang round viciously.

Snap. Scrunch.

The gander fell among the still, stricken geese. Then at last the valiant remnant turned and fled. One goose and a young gander broke from the wings of the flock. The two ran back towards the hut squawking a warning.

'Quick! Mount!'

Hygd and Sigi crawled out to meet them.

'You can't carry us,' said Hygd. 'We're too big.'

'Don't argue,' snapped the goose. 'Just get on board.'

'But what about Mai?' quavered Sigi.

'Hurry!' panted the gander.

With a despairing look at the feathers still floating over the battlefield, Hygd and Sigi jumped astride the downy steeds. With a long, labouring run, the two geese raced across the grass, launched into the air, thrust their powerful wings out into the wind and sailed above the farm. High over the hills they wheeled and flew for the north, away from Senargad.

Carrying Mai between them, the wolves sped for the trees.

13

For the third day running Princess Kara was summoned to hear her father give judgment. She dropped the silken robe she was embroidering to the floor with a cry of annoyance.

'Has the world gone mad? Who is it now?'

Elli shook her head dumbly and started to gather up the fallen sewing. The other waiting-women got to their feet, folding their work neatly. All round the princess's chamber were heaps of clothes, bed-coverings, wall-hangings. Rich wools and linens and furs fit for a queen-to-be. Kara would not go willingly to Bergenring, but she would go proudly, loaded with her father's wealth.

The women trooped behind her down the stairs and into the great beamed hall. The palace was filled with wedding-guests. Noble thanes had slept the night packed on benches and corners of the floor in this same hall. Their women had crowded into the side-chambers, displacing Kara's maids. The streets were thronged with their retainers.

Now the feasting and praise-singing and gift-giving were set aside. Guests lined the walls behind the ranks of warriors. The guards of Senargad were sober-faced, as was their custom, but the visitors were alive with curiosity.

Once more King Jarlath sat in his judgment seat. His cloak was gold, lined with black sable. Round his grizzled head was a band of serpent-circled gold. On his arms were rings of gold, heavy, garnet-studded. Even his shoes were embroidered with gold. He was the richest king of the Northern Lands, yet still hungry for more.

Once more behind him stood the Rhymester's still, dark shadow, where the light from the long windows did not penetrate.

56

Once more Princess Kara watched the oak doors swing open and the third prisoner was hounded in. She gave an exclamation of anger. Had she, the only daughter of King Jarlath, betrothed to the son of the king of Bergenring, been interrupted in her wedding-preparations for this?

This pock-marked girl. This wretched bundle of rags. This scratched, soiled, skinny wraith of a child.

The wolves herded her forward to the king, then crouched on their bellies. Their tongues lolled, their tails quivered for praise.

Jarlath beckoned forward his black-browed tenant.

'So, Witgan, son of Ari? Is this your daughter, Hygd?'

The terrified farmer shook his head.

'N-no, your Majesty! But that is very like my daughter's apron she has round her waist.'

The king sprang to his feet with a roar of anger. The wolves leaped up also with a howl of dismay. A shiver of excitement ran round the hall.

The king took a step towards the edge of the dais. Just one step, but full of menace. His voice was soft and dangerous, like the slipping of snow before an avalanche.

'Then tell me, little girl. Who are you?'

'Mai, that was Hroar's daughter, if you please. I am goose-girl in Unferthsdal.'

There was a commotion in the corner of the hall. Heads turning to stare at the noble thane, Unferth. Neighbours made jokes. Others threats. One lift of Jarlath's hand stilled them.

Kara was pale with rage.

A goose-girl! Had her father and all his guests and she herself been brought here to be mocked by a goose-girl?

The girl was shaking with fear but she kept her head up. Big violet eyes looked back at the king out of her scarred face.

The king stepped from the dais, his gold cloak slithering round him. The Rhymester was just one step behind.

'And where is Hygd, Witgan's daughter?'

'I cannot tell you that, sir. As far as my geese can carry her before they drop.'

'*Your* geese!' thundered Unferth from his corner. 'They're *my* geese, you treacherous hussy!'

Tears dropped from Mai's beautiful eyes.

'No one's geese now, for they're most of them dead.'

The wolves sank lower.

'I do not believe you.' The king was almost on her now. 'Tell me where she is, you little liar.'

'I can't, for I don't know, sire,' wept Mai. 'Truly I don't.'

'Tell me. *Tell me!*' He had her by her thin arm now. 'Tell me where they have taken her.'

'No! No!'

Women looked away. Some of the men cleared their throats awkwardly.

The Rhymester's voice hissed through the air like falling snow, soft, insistent, deadly.

> 'Let wings of fear from Jarlath's throne
> Fly those who cross our golden king
> To dungeon grim beneath the stone,
> Till Kara has wed Bergenring.'

A heavy flap cracked the autumn air. The windows darkened. The palace shook, as though something monstrous had settled on the roof. The hair on the wolves' necks bristled and the warrior's scalps rose too. A rush of cold draught as it landed in the courtyard. A shuffling of claws, then a coarse, commanding '*Caw!*'

'Take her,' whispered the Rhymester to the wolves.

They slunk down the hall, gripping the hem of her apron in yellow teeth. Mai tried to hang back, not knowing what was happening, but terrified. Her skinny limbs were no match for the powerful muscles of the wolves. Out through the swinging door they dragged her to the vast shadow that waited in the yard. The crowd craned forward to watch, half avid and half fearful. Kara stared out across their heads.

A gigantic raven, with eyes of fire like the Rhymester's wolves. A massive black beak opening on a single harsh sound. Huge, horny talons seized the helpless goose-girl. The small green apron fluttered as the two rose into the sky, casting darkness over Senargad.

14

'So, daughter! Watch, and learn obedience.'

The king turned on Kara, cruel in front of all his
staring guests. She was used to it. He had never loved
her. For three black days she had borne the weight of
his mounting anger. And because of that she must marry
the witless Oslaf.

Finnglas. Larsa. And now this scrawny goose-girl. Three
girls had dared to defy the king before all his thanes. Even
the bravest of men did not cross Jarlath of the Wolves. Yet
these three girls had faced the Wolves, and the Serpent and
the Raven, and not one of them had given way.

Kara was as proud as her father. She set her mouth
in a thin, grim line like his. Grey eyes stared back at
him, dry of tears.

'I will remember them, your Majesty.'

And she turned on her heel and walked quickly from the
hall, with her waiting-women hurrying after her.

Back in her chamber she flung herself on the fur-covered
bed.

'How can they! How dare they mock my father? That
pirate who calls herself a princess. That brawny pot-girl.
And this disgusting ragamuffin. They have made a fool
of him!'

'I shouldn't have thought that would worry you. He's
never given you any reason to love him. You'll be free of
him soon,' said Grealada, older and more insolent than the
rest of the women.

'Get out! How dare you speak to his daughter like that!'
exclaimed the princess in a towering rage. 'You presume
too much!'

The women hastened out of the door, coloured skirts fluttering. Only Elli looked back at her mistress with a troubled, kindly face.

'It's all right, Elli. You can stay,' sighed Kara. 'I'm very tired.'

As the door shut behind the others, tears sprang to her eyes. For she did love her father, had always loved him, from the time she was a tiny, motherless baby. Her grief was that he had never loved her in return, though he loaded her with riches and kept her always before his eyes.

Elli looked at her sadly but did not dare to touch her. She busied herself about the room, tidying away the wedding-trousseau. As she worked, she glanced often out of the window.

'You should rest, your Highness,' she told Kara. 'It's your wedding-day tomorrow and tonight there will be a great feast for the prince of Bergenring.'

'Oslaf!' said Kara bitterly. 'My father would marry me to a fool. And why? Because those traitors make *him* look a fool. So I must pay.'

'It's a rich kingdom you're marrying into,' Elli soothed her. 'Not rich in gold, like Senargad. But skilled in cunning.'

'The dwarves! The master-smiths beneath the mountains. They say they fashion magic into jewels.'

'And men pay dearly for that. You'll make a rich pair, my lady, with the might of your father and the magic of Bergenring.'

'And so I must be bought and sold. Do you know that, Elli? It is not the king, my father, who chiefly wants this marriage. It is the Rhymester. It is not enough for him that he has my father in his power. He wants power over every other creature too. And I am the price at which it can be bought. With a golden ring. What does he care for the human hand that must wear it?'

Elli's face softened. But before she could speak a trickle of movement outside caught her eye.

She rushed to the window.

'Bergenring! Look, my lady! The king and the prince and all their party are coming!'

Kara ran to look too, forgetting her dignity for the moment. The shuttered city was springing into life again. Crowds were rushing on to the streets, gates swinging wide, flowers strewing the ground before the lucky hooves of the bridegroom's horse.

They rode fine bay ponies. Their retinue carried ranks of steel-tipped spears. Rich furs wrapped men and women, bearskin, sealskin, arctic fox. Their king, Thidrandi, was a huge man, his black hair and black beard grizzled with silver. His cloak bore a black bear's head. But the prince beside him was like his mother, Queen Suld. So fair that his hair was almost white. Round, pale-blue eyes that stared and smiled at everything. A beardless moon-face, nodding and chuckling, as though the world was a constant source of merriment.

'My husband!' hissed Kara, like a cat.

Outside the palace gate, someone else watched the procession ride through. A stout, stocky boy in the russet tunic of a farmer's son. Bor stared, but hardly saw, as though they passed him in a dream. The fine deerskin boots, the soft sheepskin saddles, the jingling silver of their harness. Bergenring meant nothing to him. His bewildered mind was darkened by a single picture. Of a monstrous raven rising into the sky, carrying an unknown girl wearing Hygd's apron.

15

Kara sat beside her father at the high table, in the seat of honour. On Jarlath's right hand was King Thidrandi of Bergenring. And on Kara's left was the bridegroom-to-be, Prince Oslaf. His mother, Suld, had dressed him in a robe of pale-blue silk, embroidered with anemones and trimmed with white ermine. Round his blond hair was a band of silver and on his arms more rings of cunningly-wrought silversmith's work. Kara looked sideways at them and wondered if any of them were of dwarves' making. The hall was packed. Only the Rhymester was not present. He never came when there was feasting. No one had ever seen him laugh.

Oslaf was dragging something out from beneath his robe. He turned to her, grinning.

'I-I've got a present for you.'

Kara watched his hands. Her eyes gleamed with hope. What would it be? A necklace, a bracelet, a brooch? Would there be some mysterious magic in its workmanship?

He struggled to free the thing from the silken folds that were spattered now with grease and gravy. He held out his fist to her, laughing with delight.

His fingers were clutching a bunch of orange poppies. The stems were bent, the delicate petals bruised.

Kara stared at his present with disappointment and disgust. She was used to her father's rich friends giving her gifts. Ornaments of precious metals, gem-studded trinkets for a lady's chamber, fine jewelry. She was wearing some of them now. But no one had ever given her a present of flowers. Common, wayside weeds that any peasant might have picked. Costing nothing.

'Pretty.' Oslaf nodded, encouraging her to take them. 'Pretty.' He touched her hair. '*You're* pretty.'

She rose from the bench with an abrupt movement of disdain. Snatching the golden mead-cup from the table she offered it to King Thidrandi and her father. Then she went round the hall holding it out haughtily to all her father's champions and his noble guests. It was a relief to have this to do. She could not bear to sit elbow to elbow with this oaf any longer. But tomorrow, and for the rest of her life . . . Elli followed her, with soft, shy footsteps, refilling the cup each time it was emptied, which was often.

On her way back to the high table Kara paused before the open window, letting the cool air flow over her face. The city of Senargad was festive with lamps. Everywhere people were making merry for her wedding. They were glad of any excuse for drinking and laughter. Light spilled from the ale-house door, gilding the blank, black waters of the harbour.

She rested her hot head against the window frame and thought of another princess. Now she envied Finnglas. She thought of that tough, lean, wind-browned girl stealing away in Jarlath's magic ship, sailing out with the morning mist. Escaping.

She went back to her place between her father and Oslaf with a heart as heavy as the golden cup between her hands.

'Am I a coward?' Kara asked Elli as she let herself be undressed that night. 'I, Kara, daughter of Jarlath, heir to the Kingdom of the Wolves? Three times in this palace a girl has stood before my father and denied him what he wanted. Am I the only one who is afraid to say no?'

'Oh, my lady, you couldn't! You mustn't!' gasped Elli.

'Why not?' Kara snatched a half-ravelled plait out of Elli's hands. 'A foreigner, a peasant and a serf. Am I not far better than they?'

'But you'd make the king so angry! Look what happened to them. Oh, dear! It makes my heart turn cold to think of it even now.'

'They are still alive. The mountains did not fall on them, nor the sun turn black.'

'How can you say that, my lady? You saw what came for them! The Wolf-Pack and the Raven of Death and that horrible Worm. Who knows what torments they are in now?'

'Finnglas is free.'

'But the others. That little goose-girl. Oh, my lady, don't even think of it. If the Rhymester should turn his finger on you! Oh, I couldn't bear it. Besides, think of . . . '

'What?'

'Well, my lady, there's . . . there's Prince Oslaf.'

'Him! I would rather wed with a moonstruck calf!'

'But . . . forgive me, your Highness. That poor boy . . . Anyone can see he loves you.'

'Love!' Kara whirled her dress out of Elli's grasp so fast the linen tore. 'Love? What do you think I care about love!' And she dealt her maidservant a stinging slap across the cheek.

'Oh, I'm sorry, your Highness! I shouldn't have spoken. Please forgive me.' Elli cowered on the other side of the bed. 'I'll go, shall I?'

There was no answer. Elli hastily tidied the princess's clothes and scuttled away. She sat mournfully outside Kara's door like a scolded dog. She would wait until it was safe to creep back in and sleep for perhaps the last time at the foot of her mistress's bed.

Kara threw herself on to a stool in front of the window. It was true. She was afraid. Afraid of her father, but far more of her father's shadow. Of the Rhymester's glowing eyes within that hood. She knew his power too well. So she sat at the window while the night ebbed away. The last night she would spend in her childhood chamber in her father's palace. Tomorrow she must make her wedding vows to that idiot boy. And then he would ride away with her to Bergenring. To the dark mountains and the freezing fiords and the long nights of snow. While, in the Summer Land, Finnglas and the monk Niall and the cat Pangur laughed beside southern seas where their Dolphin swam. Kara was too proud to sob. But cold tears slid down her face.

16

The guests gasped when they saw Kara dressed for her wedding-day. They were finely dressed themselves. But she was magnificent. A gold-brocaded kirtle. A mantle lined with softest fur. Jewels at her neck, her arms, her hair, her waist. Even her catskin slippers were sewn with amethysts. She approached the dais loaded with all the riches of Senargad. Beneath the dazzling splendour no one noticed how pale her face was or how her fists were clenched by her sides. Oslaf started forward, crowing with admiration, and had to be hauled back by his father, Thidrandi.

King Jarlath sat on a great gold throne on the dais, gold-clad, grey-eyed, like his daughter. But today the Rhymester did not lurk behind him like a half-spied shadow. Beyond and above the king's throne reared a higher platform on a wooden scaffold. Raised above everyone the Rhymester squatted, dark-cloaked and hooded as always. No hint of gold on him. No colour. No jewels. Only the pin-point rubies of his eyes. He scanned the hall below, like an eagle from his perch, waiting for the lamb to come.

In front of the dais a low brazier had been lit. The iron knobs at its corners were grinning wolf-heads. The flames were almost invisible in the morning sunlight. But as Kara stared through its heat she saw her father's face wavering and distorted. The Rhymester's cloak swayed behind the grey smoke.

All round the fire a wide space had been left clear. Only Kara and Oslaf stood side by side before it. The princess glanced sharply from the shimmering heat to her smiling bridegroom. Did the fool understand how high they must leap to clear the unseen flames? Prince Oslaf laughed as though he hadn't a care in the world.

> 'I charge you, Prince, in Odin's name.
> To take that hand for which you came.'

Oslaf stared vacantly. Then at a sharp whisper from his mother, he shuffled closer and took Kara's long hand in his plump one. She felt she could hardly bear his touch.

Jarlath's voice sounded now, as like the Rhymester's as the crashing wave is like the slither of the undertow.

'Oslaf, Thidrandi's son, will you take Kara, Jarlath's daughter, to be your wife?'

'Yes. Oh, yes!' he babbled. He understood that.

'Kara, Jarlath's daughter, do you submit yourself to Oslaf, Thidrandi's son, to obey him as your husband?'

She felt she was suffocating. She gasped for words but no sound came. Then, with a wild gesture of fear and rage, she snatched her hand away from Oslaf.

'I will not! No, I will never wed him!'

The golden ring he had been offering her went spinning away towards the flames. There was an indrawn breath from every mouth in the hall, like a sudden gale.

The king rose, stooping his head towards her, more like a serpent than a man.

'What do you say!'

She wanted to run. She wanted to race down the long hall, down the street, out on to the harbour and the wide, trackless sea. But she was not Finnglas. She had no friends to help her. No ship waiting in the mist. What she did she must do alone.

In a low, clear voice, just a little shaky, she repeated, 'I will not wed him.'

Jarlath was coming down the steps on the other side of the fire.

'You . . . will . . . do . . . what . . . I . . . say!'

Desperately she appealed to the throng of witnesses.

'The thanes have heard me. I do not consent to this marriage.'

She was no longer looking at her father. The Rhymester had risen on his scaffold-seat. His arms spread wide, terrible as the Raven now.

Was it pride or fear that made her gasp out hastily?

'There is no need to summon monsters to fetch me. I am the king's daughter. I will go to whatever punishment you condemn me of my own free will.'

The Rhymester's finger lowered, pointing.

'Go, to lightless woe and gloom.
The steps are short, but long your doom.
Until obedience sets you free
Buried forever shall you be.'

He seemed to be staring somewhere behind her. She swung round slowly, with deliberate dignity. The door was open. The sky beyond was bright blue, a fine autumn morning. Crowds were gathered outside the gates across the empty courtyard. She walked towards the light as in a dream.

Behind her there was chaos. Thidrandi's hand had flown to his sword-hilt to avenge this insult. Bergenring's warriors were rushing for the weapons they had laid aside. The eyes of Jarlath's guard flared hungrily, their wolfhood already rising.

Oslaf's childish voice rose above the hubbub.

'Kara, where are you going? Kara, can I come too?'

The fool was crying like a boy that has lost his toy.

She walked out into the wide, windswept courtyard and breathed the keen air. How long before she felt it again?

There were pattering footsteps behind her. Kara half-turned.

'Elli! Go back! You can't follow me now.'

'Oh, no, my lady. You shan't send me away. Not this time.'

'Leave me, Elli! I order you.'

Kara quickened her step. There was a huge boulder before her. She had passed it a thousand times before. Here Jarlath's vikings sharpened their bright weapons before their

68

bloody cruises. On its summit was balanced a long shaft of rock. Thor's hammer-stone.

The rock seemed to summon her feet towards it. A long crack ran down one face. Strange that she had never noticed it before. The crack grew wider, blacker, like a tunnel opening.

The din from the hall had risen to a crescendo. A table crashed over. There was a clash of steel. But above it all, closer at hand, came the sound of heavier running feet.

'Kara, I want to come with you! Kara, wait!'

By the apples of Asgard, was she never to be free of the dolt, even here?

The sunlight showed three steps, going down into the earth. The rest was darkness. Summoning her courage, Kara darted forward into the shadow. Down one step. Two. Three.

As Thidrandi and Jarlath's hosts burst out into the yard, the lips of the boulder closed blackly around her. She shut her eyes. But she had not been quick enough. Someone else was panting in the darkness. Oslaf had crowded on to the second step behind her, and on the top step, Elli.

Below them, in the deserted harbour, a blue-black head lifted between the mooring-ropes, watching with interest. The dolphin whistled thoughtfully.

17

A trail of golden slime glistened on the loose stones beside a dark river. Larsa and Mai did go near it, but they welcomed the feeble gleam of light it gave. On either side of it the vast underground cavern was completely dark. For three days now Larsa had explored as far as the light would reach, and Mai for two days. One way they did not go. Back up the sloping passage that led towards the daylight. That way was blocked. There was no heavy, bolted door. No gate inscribed with magic runes. The tunnel was filled with the fat, black-patterned, scaly coils of the Worm, barring them from the sunlit world he could not see. From beyond came the warning sound of the Raven's 'Caw'.

The cavern seemed to rise higher above them than forest trees. It spread many times wider than King Jarlath's hall. The walls dripped dankly.

'Do you think it's safe to be drinking this water?' asked Mai, catching the drips in her hand.

'There's nothing else. It hasn't poisoned me yet,' said Larsa.

The water had an earthy taste, with a tang of metal. Neither of them wanted to try the black river. The food was worse. Stale, mildewed bread and strips of dark, dried meat. They washed the taint of the Worm from it as best they could. But even then it made them shudder.

The golden trail went on beyond the cavern. Another tunnel squeezed the river into a narrow cleft between ledges of rock. The glow vanished round a low-roofed bend deep into the mountain.

Mai peered down it and groaned, 'Well, that looks the only way left. We've tried everywhere else. No other tunnel, no door, no steps. Do you know what's down there?'

'No,' answered Larsa. 'I was leaving that till last. I don't much like the look of it. And anyway, it leads down, not up.'

'I shouldn't mind down for a change,' said Mai. 'Not as long as that beastly great Raven's still squatting up there on the mountain. I can feel her awful red eyes still watching for me.'

'I can feel something more horrible than that. I'd rather not touch anywhere that nasty Worm's been, thank you very much.' Larsa shuddered and rubbed her bare arms as though the foulness would not go away.

Mai came back and sat beside her. The two girls hugged each other. Larsa began to sing, and Mai's voice joined with hers. The music rose bravely into the vast darkness.

'All the same,' Larsa said, a little while later, 'we can't just do nothing, can we?'

The girls got up and began to creep across the cave, trying not to dislodge the shifting stones in the gloom. Larsa hung back at the mouth of the tunnel. A broad smear of slime slicked the rock ledge that was the only path. She could not bear to place her feet on it. But Mai was small and nimble. She set her bare toes down carefully between the traces, working her way forward, bending her head beneath the lowering roof.

The darkness behind Larsa deepened. A stench filled the air. Scales scraped the stones. A blind head came weaving across the cavern, blotting out the glow of its own trail.

'I s-s-see you.'

Mai froze.

'S-s-step back. That way is-s-s forbidden. All ways-s-s are forbidden. There is-s-s no way out.'

Slowly Mai edged back into the wide, dank cave. The little hand that gripped Larsa's was shivering.

'S-s-stay s-s-still. I s-s-see you.'

'He doesn't really,' murmured Larsa. 'He just senses us.'

'That's almost worse. It means he can find us even in the dark.'

They heard the Worm dragging his way back up the tunnel.

71

'All the same,' said Larsa when he had gone. 'His trail leads down there. Why? There must be something round that bend.'

'Do you think it's treasure? Isn't that what dragons guard in the stories?'

'Whose treasure? I wonder where we are.'

'The Raven carried me north over a great plain with lakes and forests. Then it started to get hilly. I could see mountains ahead covered with black fir trees and snow shining on their peaks. She came down on one of the lower ones, beside a dark lake. There was this cave and the dreadful Worm inside, and then . . . oh, Larsa, I found you!'

'It was night when the Worm brought me here. But what you saw sounds like the tales they tell of Bergenring.'

'There won't be dwarves, will there? Not on top of everything else?'

Larsa laughed and squeezed her hand. 'Cheer up. You've faced up to the Wolves and the Raven and the Serpent. Surely even dwarves would be a nice change after them?'

'I hope it isn't treasure. It was gold that got us here. I'd much rather it was the way home.'

'Come on. We're still alive, aren't we?'

'Till the princess's wedding day.'

'Mai.'

'Yes?'

'That's today.'

There was little else left to say.

'Larsa. We've got to get out of here. I couldn't face the Rhymester again.'

'I know. Nor could I. He'd make me tell him about Erc.'

'I haven't got enough courage, Larsa. What can we do?'

'Let me think.'

'If I kept the Worm busy while you . . . '

'If he went to sleep . . . '

Their voices trailed away. It was hopeless.

From outside came the loud cry of the Raven. There was an indrawn hiss of serpent's breath. A long shudder heaved through the stones. The river gurgled as if a pot-hole had opened somewhere in its depths.

Mai clutched Larsa. 'Whatever is it?'

'Never mind what it is. Now! Before he realizes we've gone.'

And Larsa sped away into the downward tunnel, dragging Mai with her. A brief rattle of wet shingle and they were on silent rock, running beside the river. Larsa no longer cared about the Worm's slimy trail. Heads stooping, they raced for the bend and the darkness beyond.

Around the corner Larsa almost fell headlong. The river dropped with a booming roar and disappeared in the darkness. Beside it, a flight of steps led steeply down.

The girls ran down the stair. There was gravelly sand under their bare feet. Their panting breath echoed back to them hollowly, as though from the walls of a long chamber. Ahead, the gleaming trail ended in shadows. The shadows were moving nearer.

18

Larsa was running too fast to stop herself. She cannoned into something cool and soft. There was a hiss of anger, a stifled scream, a chuckle.

'Get back! How dare you!' A voice high with rage.

Larsa stumbled backwards, almost knocking over Mai, who was hiding behind her.

The golden glow rose feebly from the floor. It gleamed on gold-brocaded cloth. The swing of another embroidered skirt. A further sparkle of silver.

Larsa's eyes came back to the first shadowy figure. She raised them from slippers studded with amethysts. A border of silky fur. To jewel-threaded plaits, encircled with a band of gold, wolf-headed.

'But you're . . . !' She gasped, bobbing a curtsy out of habit as her voice trailed away in amazement.

'The Princess Kara. And . . . ' Kara spat the words. 'Prince Oslaf of Bergenring.'

Mai came forward, scratching her tangled hair. 'But . . . if you please, your Highness . . . what are you doing down here? This is your wedding-day!'

'You are wrong,' replied Kara haughtily. 'I did not choose to be wed.'

'I'm going to marry her!' Oslaf nodded his fair head eagerly.

'Sh!' soothed Elli.

'But how . . . why . . . ?' Larsa struggled to understand.

'Has your father thrown you in prison for a punishment, like us?' Mai asked.

'A princess is not *thrown*! I came of my own free will. Do you think you are the only two with courage and pride? Is a princess not braver than a potter and a goose-girl? But these two followed me here against my orders. And you? What were you doing when you stumbled against me so rudely? What danger threatens?'

'We . . .'

'We were . . .'

'Escaping.'

'Excuse me, your Highness.' Mai was edging round Kara. 'But is that the way out?'

Even as she spoke, a voice began to hiss from the roof, from the walls, from the water.

'I s-s-see you!'

Elli gave another scream that smothered Kara's gasp. Larsa and Mai clutched each other. Only Oslaf looked round, smiling and unafraid.

'Run!' cried Larsa, taking control of her fear. She rushed past Elli and Oslaf.

'Run, your Highness!' said Mai, darting after her.

'A princess does not run!' snapped Kara. 'Stay!' she commanded Elli and Oslaf. 'We cannot escape our doom.'

The two girls pelted on into the shadows. The floor was shelving upwards. The golden path split suddenly into many tracks, like a branching tree.

'Which way?' gasped Larsa.

'This one's the biggest,' called Mai, running on.

The cave became a tunnel. The slope grew ever steeper. Now it was a flight of high stone steps. They panted up it, hearts hammering. Mai checked suddenly.

The tip of a spear-pointed tail coiled round the corner. Black arrow markings on green knife-edged scales.

A soft, sibilant voice whispered around them, 'I s-s-see you!'

Dumb with fear they doubled back and tried a smaller branch. A hard, hooked claw. A spreading foot. A crouching leg.

'You s-s-see?'

'It's no good,' moaned Larsa as they stumbled back into the gravelled cave. 'They're everywhere.'

75

'Are there lots of them . . . it?' whispered Mai. 'Or is it always the same one?'

'*In serpent-circled dark forlorn.*' Larsa shuddered. 'He meant it, didn't he?'

Three shadowy figures waited motionless where the river plunged.

'You see? A princess always knows best,' said Kara loftily. 'We cannot escape.'

She moved to sit down, as though suddenly tired. Oslaf snatched off his mantle and threw it on the sand behind her. She sank on to it without a word of thanks. A moment later she sprang up, clutching the back of her dress.

'You pigeon-headed loon! You put it over a puddle!'

'It doesn't matter,' said Mai, helping Elli squeeze out the water. 'Everything here is as wet as weeping.'

Kara lowered herself again, more cautiously. She nodded graciously to the others.

'You may sit too.'

Larsa and Mai looked at each other with raised eyebrows.

'But I still don't understand,' said Larsa. 'How did you get in that way? Who brought you here?'

'A king's daughter does not have to be brought. I chose to walk.'

'There were steps going deep down into the earth,' said Elli. 'It was horrible.'

'We went into the weapon-stone!' exclaimed Oslaf, drawing his short sword and waving it about. 'Snick! Snack!'

'But you couldn't have walked all this way!' said Larsa. 'That's not possible. We must be almost in Bergenring.'

'A princess does not lie! Our way seemed short. But it was weary.'

Mai looked around her and shivered.

'I wonder where we really are.'

The dreaded voice seemed to drip from the walls.

'Is-s-s it not obvious-s-s? You are in the Borderlands-s-s. The laws-s-s of the world above do not run here. S-s-some paths to it are s-s-short and s-s-some s-s-seem long. S-s-some

76

come to it through love, others-s-s from hate. The ways-s-s to enter it are many. But no roads-s-s lead out. There is-s-s no es-s-scape. Des-s-spair!'

'A princess is always right,' said Kara. 'We must stay here until the Rhymester summons us. We have no choice.'

'But we can't just wait! As soon as you are married he's going to drag us back.'

'Question us till he gets what he wants.'

'Terrify us.'

'Torture us.'

'But . . . you didn't get married!'

'Nor will I ever, to Oslaf. A princess does not change her mind.'

'Then . . . what will happen to us now?'

'I think there will be a war between Senargad and Bergenring,' Kara said calmly. 'We may have a long time to wait.'

They sat in silence on the wet sand, each wrapped in their own thoughts. After a while Kara turned to Larsa.

'Of course, it is different for you. You are not a princess. If my father threatens you again, you will tell him the traitor's name.'

The pot-girl's face burned red under the cover of darkness.

'I'd rather die first! But it's easy to say that, sitting here. None of us knows how brave we will be until the moment comes.'

'I'm not brave at all,' shuddered Elli. 'If anyone so much as lifted a finger to me, I'd give in at once. I know I would.'

'Common coward! You were not reared to be a princess. No one will ever persuade me to marry Prince Oslaf, whatever they do,' scoffed Kara. ' . . . And you? Will you not tell my father where Hygd is if he tortures you?'

'How can I?' cried Mai. 'How can I tell him what I don't know?'

Larsa sat up suddenly and stared at her.

'You mean you weren't just pretending? You *really* don't

77

know what's happened to Sigi and Hygd? Haven't you any idea?'

'To tell you the truth,' confessed Mai, 'I didn't actually believe those geese could fly.'

19

Hygd thrust her hands into the soft neck feathers of Brodd, the grey goose. She felt the strong breast straining to flap outspread wings. Brodd's orange beak speared forward as though gasping in the rushing air. Beside her, Sigi's long legs dangled below Odd, the gander. Poor Odd was sinking ever lower under the weight.

'Go, goosey, go!' urged Hygd.

They swept through the cool, blue air. Over heaths speckled white with sheep. Over lakes brim-full of cloudless sky. Over birchwoods that were beginning to turn yellow. Over the dark green spires of the spruce forests. The sky was growing greyer. The hills becoming higher. The valleys narrowing, darkening.

'Oh, dear! Oh, my! I can't go much further. I shall have to sit down,' wheezed Brodd.

'Thank goodness for that! I thought you were never going to say. I'm fit to drop,' Odd croaked.

'That's right. Blame me. Just like a gander. You could have stopped first. But, oh no. It has to be me that's the one to give up.'

'I was only doing my best. I've got responsibilities.'

'Oh, yes! So have we all . . . Odd? . . . Odd!'

The gander had plummeted out of sight. Hygd leaned over.

'There he is!'

Odd was spiralling earthwards like a grey, falling leaf. His exhausted wings could barely flap. Sigi was clinging on to his drooping neck.

'Hold tight, ducky!'

Brodd dived after them.

A lake was rushing up to meet them. Still, dark grey waters, ringed with forests. A single, stony island, close to the shore. On it, a castle, with a single tower. Its walls were hung with curved wooden tiles, the gables upswept like the prow of a ship, each ending in a carved bear's head.

Brodd's wings swept back, blotting the view from Hygd's face. There was a shower of spray. Pink feet skidding over the surface. Brodd settled on the lake amidst rings of spreading ripples.

Odd was a raft of dishevelled feathers nearby. His head was tucked under one weary wing. From him came a whistling snore.

'Of course,' Brodd said kindly. 'He was carrying a bigger handicap.'

Sigi tumbled off Odd's back and waded ashore. Brodd paddled into the shallows until Hygd could join him.

When the last ripples had wandered away into the reeds the lake was motionless. A thrush tapped a snail against a stone. The sound rang like a hammer in a quarry.

At evening the wild, barred barnacle geese came drifting down on to the lake like an early snowfall.

20

Bor bolted. Already there was fighting in the streets of Senargad. He dodged round it. He wanted no part of it. Somehow he felt that it was his fault, though he could not understand how.

Before he was clear of the city a train of horse-riders swept past him. King Thidrandi, black beard flying, Queen Suld, and those of their followers who had escaped. With a bellow, 'The Bear of Bergenring shall avenge this!' they swung their steeds on to the northern road and galloped away.

Bor's father came home in an evil mood. Next day mailed men came for him and thrust a spear into his hand. He marched away with Jarlath's host. Bor and his mother, Gerda, were left alone.

As the days shortened, and the air thickened, and the frost lingered in the grass, Bor walked down to the beach many times. He stood on the edge of the sound, looking out at the endless grey sea.

'Tell me!' he shouted into the wind. 'Why don't you tell me what to do?'

But Arthmael did not answer him again.

The armies clashed. The Rhymester sat in his tent, crouched on his magician's scaffold. His power unleashed the Wolves. Under the drawn hood his mind was concentrated, holding and directing the king and all his hosts by its spell. Men said that at the head of Bergenring's army marched a grim black bear who could kill ten warriors with a single blow of his paw.

The news spread even to the sad cave-mouth of the Borderlands. With a cry of 'War! War!' the Raven of Battle rose on giant wings that darkened the sky. She flew south and hung over the armies, scouring the battlefield for the newly-dead. Her dark beak dripped red.

Fierce the fighting, bitter the bloodshed. Many brave men fell. Day after day the land rocked with battle. So black was the anger of Jarlath and Thidrandi that they did not notice the first speckle of snow on the trampled ground.

Next morning they woke in their tents and booths and found the snowdrifts had built high ramparts between them.

On that same dawn, in the far islands north of Britain, Erc climbed on to the deck of Jarlath's stolen ship. There was ice on the rigging.

'We must hurry,' he said to Finnglas. 'The seas are closing.'

And over them all, in V-shaped skeins across the sky, flew the barnacle geese. They raced the north wind, going south before the storms of winter.

Part 2

21

On the first day of summer Finnglas was crowned queen. A week ago, after long voyaging, she had come home and held her dying father in her arms. For seven dangerous nights the warriors, bards and druids of the Summer Isle had tested her, to see if she was fit to be their queen. Then, as the sun rose on the first morning of May, the whole tribe hailed her, 'Finnglas! Finnglas of the Horses! Finnglas is our queen!' The ancient Stones of Choosing on the hill rang with her name and Arthmael himself leaped out of the ocean to share their rejoicing.

Now her coronation day was ending with feasting and laughter. Up at the stronghold of Rath Daran, long tables had been set under the stars. The young queen's guests had eaten well, and still the wine went round the circle. Finnglas sat amongst the noblest of the Summer Land. Tomméné, her master of horses, Manach, leader of her hosts, Sorcha Clear-Sight, wise in the ways of the heavens, and Laidcenn, Chief Bard. Further down the table one figure stood out from all the rest. Niall, in his plain monk's robe among all the flash of finery and fire of jewels. He took a harp of his own crafting and sang a song he had made for Finnglas. On the bench beside him sprawled Pangur the cat. His stomach was round and full with good food and milk. He opened one eye as Niall's rich voice began singing, then fell asleep.

But when Niall came back to the bench, the place on his other side was empty. One of Finnglas's friends was missing.

On a beach of the Summer Isle, just off the coast of Ireland, a boy from the Northlands walked moodily. There was no sunshine now to catch the fire of his red hair or the freckles of his face. The sun had long since set, but light still lingered in the pale sky as though it did not want this day of happiness to end.

As the wind blew warm from the south, Erc sighed. What was a poor fisherman's son doing amongst nobles like these? Young Rohan, the bright charioteer, clashing with gold and armour. Girl-druids, learning from the wise Sorcha the mathematics of the East. Boys skilled in fencing, hunting, gaming, who could still tune a harp sweetly and tell old tales of honour. All day they had crowded round Finnglas. She had given gifts to everyone. They called her 'Gold-Giver', 'Peace-Weaver', 'Lady of Horses.'

But what was Erc? Once he had set Finnglas free from the prison tower in Senargad. Once he had ferried her through the mist in his fishing boat. Once he had sailed away with her in King Jarlath's ship. Those days of adventure were over. He was nothing here, and Finnglas was queen.

He lifted his eyes and found the friendly Pole Star, just beginning to prick through the evening sky. His practised sailor's gaze went round the heavens naming the stars. As they moved past the Maiden a thread of movement caught his eye. A double skein of shadows was winging slowly across the almost colourless heavens, coming up out of the south. He heard the heavy beat of their flight above the lapping of the sea. His heart twisted with envy. The winter was over. The wild geese were flying home.

But as the evening darkened the leader dipped his long neck seawards and the whole convoy came gliding down in V-shaped formation, like an arrow aimed at Erc's heart. He watched their wings thrust back, their feet kick up the spray, their feathers settle as they folded themselves for sleep on the waters of the bay.

Erc walked out across the rocks towards them. They were barnacle geese. White-faced, black-headed, bodies barred with grey and black.

'Greetings,' he said shyly.

'And peace to you,' they crooned.

'Where are you going?'

86

'North, with the winds of summer.'

'Tell me,' Erc asked longingly. 'Have you ever seen Senargad?'

'Last spring we spent in Senargad, and the summer in Bergenring. At autumn we flew south, over the Borderlands.'

'What did you see? What news do you have of it?'

At once there rose a clucking so loud that if there had not been such merrymaking in Rath Daran they would have heard it even in the hill-fort. The wild geese told a strange tale.

Erc burst into the firelight. Every other face was flushed, but his was pale. He rushed towards the high table, but Finnglas's seat was empty. The pipes were skirling and the drums beat an insistent rhythm. All round him young men and women were dancing. Kilts flew and skirts swirled. Jewels flashed in the firelight and died in the shadows. A circle of gold swung into the light, on long brown hair threaded with pearls. Laughing hazel eyes. Her partner jingled with jewelry like a horse's harness. Finnglas was dancing with her cousin, Rohan.

'Finnglas!' Erc panted without ceremony. 'I've got to speak to you.'

'A new reign indeed,' tall Rohan stopped dancing and raised his eyebrows, 'when a fisherman's son can interrupt a queen!'

'Have a care what you say, cousin.' Finnglas's eyes flashed dangerously. 'I hold Erc, Erc's son, nobler than any warrior here. I owe him my life and my honour.'

She took Erc's arm and walked away with him into the shadows, leaving the trinketed chariot-champion speechless. Away from the fire, it was not wholly dark even yet. The pale memory of day had faded, but the air was luminous as though the whole hillside lay waiting for the moon.

Finnglas stood, breathing deeply, gazing out to sea and letting the wind cool her cheeks.

'Well, go on. Tell me. What news is so urgent that it cannot wait till morning on this, the day of my crowning?'

Erc's voice came low and stumbling.

'I have made a dreadful mistake. My father is dead and my mother was sold here as a slave. When I helped you escape from Jarlath I thought I could sail away with you and start a new life. I truly believed I had nothing left in Senargad. No family. No home. I thought no one could be hurt by what I did. But I was wrong. Terribly wrong. Two girls are in dreadful danger because of me. Even the king's own daughter is in prison. And two small children I knew, Sigi and Hygd, are even now . . . Oh, Finnglas! I've got to go back and free them!'

'Gently, Erc. I cannot understand this. Rein in the wild horses of your tongue and tell me the whole story properly.'

Erc drew a deep breath and began to unfold the tale the barnacle geese had told him. A dark tale of wolves and serpents and ravens. Of faithfulness and treachery. Of enchantment and war. Of a castle in a lake.

As he finished the silver moon was rising over the sea, laying a long, glittering road across the water. The light fell on three more figures seated behind them, listening and watchful. The young monk Niall, the plump white cat, Pangur Bán, and Erc's mother, Ranvaig, freed now from slavery in Finnglas's land.

Finnglas seized Erc's hand.

'Nobly spoken, Erc! As always. It is because of us they are in danger now. Shall we sport here, feasting and dancing while our friends suffer? Come! I take the first adventure of my reign! Who will follow me to Senargad?'

She whipped her royal sword out of its scabbard.

'I will! Gladly!' cried Niall.

Erc's mother, Ranvaig, spoke softly out of the shadows. 'You are forgetting, Finnglas. You are not a wild princess now, but a queen. And newly-made. There were those who did not wish to see you crowned. You still have many enemies. Your task is here, to hold this land in peace.'

Finnglas gasped a protest. 'Would you dishonour me?'

But Niall's hand fell steadying on her shoulder.

'Ranvaig is right. You are not free to please yourself. A queen's crown sits heavier than a princess's coronet. So

Arthmael warned you. And where you are, I must be. I swore on your father's deathbed I would stay beside you.'

In the long silence they felt Finnglas battling with herself. Then the sword slowly rasped back into its scabbard of healing. Her voice was gruff as she grasped Erc's arm.

'It grieves me more than words can say to lose such a dear friend. But if what you tell is true, then you can no longer stay with honour. Yet I cannot bear to let you go into danger alone. It was for me you have risked and lost so much already.'

The white cat stretched and yawned and began to wash behind his ears. His purr rumbled from the moonlit grass at their feet.

'Don't worry, Erc. If Finnglas and Niall are too busy to help you, *I'll* come with you and rescue your friends.'

The others stared down at Pangur Bán as he licked the taste of supper from between his toes.

'By the way,' asked Pangur. 'How are we going to get back to Senargad?'

Erc found his voice. 'At dawn the barnacle geese will be flying home.'

22

The Northlands lay locked in the grip of a winter so hard that even the coming of May could not release them. Bergenring suffocated under a weight of frozen snow that choked its narrow valleys and broke the backs of the fir trees. Grey skies frowned low over Senargad on the hummocks of houses hidden under drifts. The sound was a field of sunless ice, snow-covered.

Golden-Spring and Bilberry chewed at the last of the mouldy hay, like the other byre-bound animals. Gerda forced the door open a chink and peered out, sad and silent. Witgan had not come home. Somewhere, no one knew where, two armies lay, imprisoned by winter. Did they dice and shiver and grumble as they waited for spring to set the rivers running? Or were they lying, stiff and frozen as last year's logs, not needing each other's swords to finish them off?

The wild geese came in low, swooping down to the sound. They checked suddenly, wings whirling wildly as the hard ice met their skating feet. The air was raucous with their angry clucking as they waddled up and down.

'Preposterous!'

'I never heard of such a thing!'

'Snow in May!'

'Why didn't somebody tell us? We could have stayed in Ireland.'

A seal slid across the ice and winked at them.

'They say Arthmael has a flipper in this. Don't ask me why.'

Erc and Pangur climbed stiffly off their mounts and thanked them warmly. Erc was blue with cold. His teeth were chattering.

'Let's go to my house. I've a few more clothes there . . . If the king hasn't seized them, like he does everything else.'

'Is it safe?' Pangur's startled eyes looked up. His white fur was almost lost in the snow. Only his green eyes showed unnaturally bright.

'Only the Sea-Wolves know it was me that rescued Finnglas . . . oh, all right, Pangur, *you* and me . . . They saw my face, but they don't know my name. If we keep out of their way, we'll be all right.'

'The two girls found out, didn't they? Larsa and Hygd. It's been a long time since the barnacle geese flew south. A lot may have changed since then.'

Erc's face flushed. 'I know Larsa. My heart wants to say that she would never tell. But how can you expect even the bravest to remain silent if they torture her? You're right, Pangur. We'll go carefully.'

While the people of Finnglas's land still laughed and danced in the summer evening, night fell quickly in clouded Senargad. The sun had never appeared. Erc and Pangur stole through the frosty shadows towards the fishermen's cottages. Pangur was wrapped round Erc's neck like a fur muffler.

Erc's feet slipped on an icy boulder. He stumbled forward with a low curse. Pangur's claws dug sharply into his neck. There was a swift movement in the shadow of a rock nearby. An intake of breath. Then silence. Both sides froze into immobility. Wondering who else was haunting the foreshore in the cold and the dark. And why.

At last the other shadow spoke. The voice quivered a little with fear and chill.

'Wh-who's there?'

Pangur felt Erc's neck muscles tense. There was a hesitation. Then he whispered, 'Can that truly be Bor? Witgan's son?'

A short, stocky figure came out of the shadow, a silhouette against the white wilderness of the sound. His voice sounded dry now, with a sort of gasp in it.

'Who . . . are you?'

'Oh, Bor! By all that's fortunate! Of all the people in Senargad, you are the only one we could be sure of now to help us. Don't you recognize me, Bor? It's me! Erc.'

There was another silence. He had expected the younger boy to come running to him. But Bor answered in a choked, helpless tone.

'Oh, why did you have to come back? Why? Why?'

And he burst into uncontrollable sobs.

Erc put his arm round Bor and comforted him. Soon he had the whole story out of him. Or so it seemed to Erc and Pangur. After all, his tears were not surprising. He had lost his father, his brother and two sisters. Erc learned that there was no news of any of them.

'And of us?' he asked, a little disappointed that no one was talking of what he had done. 'Do they know it was me that got Finnglas away?'

Bor shook his head. 'They know about the white cat,' he said, stroking Pangur and sniffing. 'But not you.'

'Not even a description? Didn't the Sea-Wolves say what I looked like? Haven't they been searching for someone like me?'

'They may be. It all changed so quickly. Lots of the wolves were drowned. And by the time the rest got back there was such an uproar at the palace over the wedding. Now nobody dares do anything without the king and . . . the Rhymester. And they've all gone to war. I don't suppose they'll ever come back.' He sounded as though he might start crying again.

'Aren't any of the Guard left? There must be someone in charge.'

'I've seen three wolves. They say that as men they were Harbard Graybeard, Thorvild the Black, and Ref Blood-Tongue.'

He did not say that as wolves these three had hunted Hygd.

'And you. What were you doing on the beach at nightfall, in this weather?'

'I . . . dug a hole in the ice. I was watching it.'

'Fishing?'

Erc walked down to the bottom of the beach and surveyed Bor's work with a fisherman's eye. A wide black hole gaped in the glimmering ice-sheet.

'But it's huge! What on earth were you expecting? Whales?'

Bor shook his head in silence. Erc cast him a sideways, troubled look. Then he laughed.

'We're freezing. Can you find us a safe bed somewhere? Then perhaps you can fetch me some more clothes in the morning. I'd better not be seen myself.'

Bor led them home. He went in first and waited till his mother had greeted him and turned back to the fire. Then, to the newcomers' surprise, he beckoned them quickly through the door and pointed up the ladder to the hayloft.

Next morning they woke to the first gleam of sunshine for months. It melted the tips of the massive icicles. Then the grey, unfriendly clouds closed in again, and the frost returned.

Bor was up early. He walked back along the shore towards the city. All the time he was glancing at the sea, as if he expected some power to come bursting up through the ice, scattering the snow to the sky. But the bay lay still and silent.

It was easy for Bor to enter Erc's house unobserved. Few people stirred out-of-doors. He had to dig away the snow around the door. He gathered up an armful of Erc's clothes, then stood in the doorway. His eyes went to the palace, with its golden wolf-heads, then back to the distant gable of his own farm. Backwards and forwards. As though he swayed between one decision and another. And most of all to the sea between them, as though he longed to find his answer there.

He had not told Erc about the chest of gold.

24

Erc carried a strange load slung on his back. It was a leather satchel, such as a travelling bard might use for his harp, or a smith for his tools. But inside this one crouched a small white cat. Pangur Bán did not poke his head out of the overhanging flap. It was not the bitter cold that kept him lying low. They knew too much here about a white cat.

Erc had pulled the hood of his cloak well forward over the tell-tale red hair. There were mittens on his hands and woollen trousers bound close about his legs. On his feet he wore Bor's gift, taken down from the rafters in the stable. Skis. Long runners of planed wood, strapped to his boots with deerskin thongs. As a fisherman, Erc had had little use for such things. But now he was finding he could move swiftly and easily over the deep, frozen snow.

'Can't you come with us, Bor? After all, it's your sisters and brother we're trying to rescue,' Erc had asked many times.

'Somebody's got to stay with my mother,' was all Bor would say.

He was walking with them now, eyes flicking nervously from side to side. What if the wolves came upon them, here, too soon? What if they stopped and challenged Erc to reveal himself? What if Bor was caught in the company of traitors? There would be not even one chest of gold then, only prison, or worse.

He accompanied them quickly round the outskirts of the town and saw them on the way to the north, though the road lay buried deep under the snow. He had urgent business in Senargad, though his friends did not know it. He watched

Erc's figure dwindle to a speck across the snow and turned back to the sea.

He had thought he would start to run then, with long, sliding strides. They mustn't get too far away from Senargad and perhaps be lost in a fresh fall of snow. Erc would never suspect Bor of treachery. It would just seem to be bad luck. A too-vigilant wolf-patrol, guarding the boundaries of Jarlath's city. And Erc would never betray the friend who had sheltered him.

All the same, his feet moved more slowly than he had planned, shuffling him towards the half-empty town.

He stiffened suddenly. He wouldn't need to go to the palace, after all. Wolves were coming across the snow towards him.

There were three of them. He recognized them. The brindled Harbard Graybeard. Thorvild, blacker than a fir-tree's shadow. Ref, panting. That moment of fear that he could never still, remembering how they had swept past him in pursuit of Hygd. He experienced that feeling that all humans knew when they saw the Rhymester's Wolves, of wanting to run but being too frightened to move.

The wolves advanced closer, a little awkwardly, for they were heavy enough to sink some way into the snow. Their breath smoked and he could hear the rasp of their throats, just a little too eager.

'Who are you? What are you doing here?' barked Harbard.

Now that the moment had come, Bor's mouth was dry. 'I . . .'

'Yes?'

Thorvild had moved round behind him. His low growl made Bor jump.

'I was on my way to the city.' The words came fast, as though he was guilty and afraid, instead of coming to give them what they wanted.

'For what? Your hands are empty. You've nothing to sell.'

Ref had come up on his other side. He was ringed by wolves.

'Some news.'

This wasn't how he had imagined it. It was as if they were forcing the words out of him. He had seen himself walking into the palace with his head held high. With a secret to sell, worth ten chests of gold. Not just a name, but the traitor himself, here in Senargad.

Yet, in spite of himself, his eyes went over their heads to the grey glimmer of the bay, the ice locked around the rocks, the lively waters frozen.

'News! What news?'

'I . . .'

He thought at first he was dreaming it. He had waited so long to see it. All through this awful, bitter winter of silence and doubt. And now, when he had at last given up all hope, when the words of betrayal were already half out of his mouth, it was there. A long, sleek muscular body rising from the sound as if the ice was nothing to it. Straight up, till it seemed that even the clouds above must part before him. Spiralling now, flipping over into a somersault, diving precisely back through the hole he had made.

Bor stared at the space where Arthmael had been. As though the sunless snow was dazzling white. As though the sky was riven blue. As though all the joy in the world were in that moment's dancing. And he was left standing in dark, frozen shadow. His mouth was open and his eyes were blurred with tears.

'Well? Spit it out, boy. What news?' Harbard's mouth was so close Bor could feel the reek of his breath.

Bor came back to his surroundings as though from a long flight. But it didn't seem like reality now. Just a bad dream. He shook his head, trying to remember what he had been saying. He didn't feel afraid now, just bewildered.

'News. You were going to tell us some news,' snapped Ref. His jaws were very close to Bor's leg.

'No! I was going to the city to *get* news. My father's with the king's army. We haven't heard of him all winter. I wanted to find if there was any news.'

'No. Use your brain. They won't be back until this snow thaws.' His voice was rough and a dark look passed between the wolves as though there was a blacker possibility.

Ref's gaze went past Bor, to a tiny distant speck in the snow.

'I spy a stranger coming!'

The Wolf-Guard's ears pricked up. The hair on their necks rose. They grew menacingly tall.

'A traveller? Coming south, out of *that*?'

Three pairs of eyes stared hungrily over the snowy wastes. Then Harbard spoke.

'No! I see tracks going away from Senargad. Starting from *here*.'

Three pairs of red-rimmed eyes swung back to Bor.

25

The snow slope rose in front of Erc. Only the width of the space between the trees showed that the road went this way. He climbed the ridge and moved more freely down the other side. The huddled roofs of Senargad were hidden from view. So was the sea.

He was skiing through a trackless, motionless, uninhabited wilderness. He slid the satchel round from his back to his chest and opened the flap. After a little pause, Pangur Bán's white head peeped out. He looked round carefully and drew a breath of the sharp air.

'Are we alone?'

'Very.'

Erc felt better now with the furry presence of Pangur in front of him. Just for a moment as he crossed the ridge the world of the Northlands had seemed a very lonely place.

'I don't wish to seem critical, Erc, but where are we going?'

'North. The way the Worm and the Raven went.'

'But if Jarlath's whole army can't move, how will we be able to?'

'We're moving now, aren't we? We'll worry about that if it gets worse. Till then, we just keep on as far as we can. After all, by the calendar, it should be spring.'

'It doesn't *feel* like spring.'

A little further on.

'Why doesn't the Rhymester do something about this snow? He seemed to be able to do anything he wanted.'

'I don't think the Rhymester *does* anything himself. He just makes other people do what he wants. From the king downwards. Even the Worm and the Raven and Wolves are in his power. That's the horrible thing about him. He changes people.'

'So does Arthmael.'

'That's different!'

'Of course, it's different. As different as heaven and hell. When Arthmael changes you, he sets you free to be what you always dreamed you could be.'

They travelled in silence for a while, with only the swish of Erc's skis carrying them on. Pangur sank deeper down into his resting-place, out of reach of the cold wind. Suddenly he leaped up, making the bag bang against Erc's chest.

'Erc! I've thought of something terrible. We've got to stop and go back.'

'Don't be silly. We were lucky to get away without being spotted. I'm not going back to Senargad till we've rescued my friends.'

'But I've just remembered. We left in such a hurry we never stopped to ask Arthmael for advice. What if we're going the wrong way? What if everything we're doing is a mistake?'

There was the briefest pause. Then Erc said, just a little too quickly, 'How can it be a mistake? He'd want us to find Hygd and set Larsa free, wouldn't he?'

'Yes. But is this the right way to do it? What if we get lost in the snow? Or stumble across Jarlath and an army of wolves? Or miss their prison completely and just go on for ever? Finnglas and Niall would never have rushed off without asking him, would they?'

'Shut up! If we get into difficulties, we'll ask Arthmael then. He'd always help us if we were in real trouble.'

'Open your eyes, Erc. Look where we are. Miles inland. Arthmael's a dolphin. How *can* he help us here?'

Could it be true? Were they really beyond the reach of Arthmael's help now? It was a chill thought. Erc skied on, faster than ever. Pangur swayed and bumped uncomfortably in his sack. At last he sighed and mewed.

'Oh, well. Arthmael has a way of using even people's mistakes. It's just that it's usually a lot more unpleasant for everyone than if they'd followed his way from the beginning.'

Erc swung the satchel round on to his back, rather more violently than was necessary.

'Do you mind? It wasn't very comfortable that way.'

He trudged on, without speaking, jolting Pangur at every step. The day, that had never been truly light since the ray of dawn sunshine, grew steadily darker. Pangur Bán peered out again and gave a loud gasp.

'I think we're being followed!'

26

In the May sunshine Finnglas and her guests hunted and
raced and cheered the wrestlers and the hurly players. At
night they danced and feasted and their eyes grew bright
in the firelight at the songs of the harpers. But morning
and evening Finnglas would slip away from the crowd to sit
alone at the water's edge, looking and listening. She smiled
as she heard Niall's lusty voice bellowing a psalm from
the rocks nearby.

The sun did not shine on the snow of the far Northlands.
There was no dancing. Under a cold May moon the wolves
howled. These were not shy forest creatures, but the Rhymester's Wolf-Guard, howling for lost homes and families, and
for their own lost selves. Yet after the howl came a long
drawn-out growl. Of hate and greed. Even as men, there had
been a part of them that longed to be wolves.

All the Rhymester's power was bent on keeping them
so. Witgan and all the other spear-carriers lay burrowed
in deep winter sleep. Shrews, hedgehogs, bats, slugs, that
could slumber unfed until he roused them for war again.
The trouble was keeping the wolves away from them as they
ranged the birchwood in search of blood. Hares, pheasants,
even the startled deer that dared show themselves fell victim
to the yellow fangs. They howled to go home. But as long as
Thidrandi's armies lay camped in the lands of Senargad, so
long must the Rhymester hold Jarlath's host ready to drive
them back when the snow thawed.

He had tried to turn his enchantment against the Black
Bear's army. He thought with a cruel smile that he would
make them butterflies and watch them start and flutter and
die in a few freezing seconds. But his spell turned back

102

sharply upon him, like a sword that has rebounded from a fine coat of mail. As indeed it had. The dwarves had forged Thidrandi's host coats that armoured more than flesh and blood. For a moment the Rhymester staggered and clutched his belly as though a blade had pierced him. He did not try that weapon on them again.

Yet that endless winter was hard even for a powerful magician like him. He grew very weary. Sometimes the red eyes dulled almost to embers, and his head fell forward. Then the wolves stirred uneasily in their sleep, flexing their paws as though they were fingers beginning to grope and feel. The king tossed in his bed of furs and murmured, 'Kara!' With an effort of will the Rhymester grasped his staff and locked his circle of power around them again. On the massive branch of a fir tree nearby the giant Raven sat huddled and bad-tempered, growing thinner every day as she waited till she could feast on battle-blood once more. The magician had no energy or thought to spare for what was happening in the Borderlands.

Snow blocked the entrance to the cave, so that even the cold-blooded Worm retreated deeper into his dank tunnel. Inside the prisoners' cavern it had never been warm, but nor did the freezing grip of winter penetrate. Month followed month in the same endless, dripping chill. After Yule there was not even the mildewed bread to eat, only the black, foul-smelling strips of dried meat. Gradually Larsa and Mai grew as pale as the princess herself, and Oslaf's face looked less like the round moon. All of them began to be racked with coughs that bent them double and drove daggers through their ribs.

But Larsa would not let them despair. Each day, as hope dwindled, she made them sing. The thin brave sound, of sun and sea and of a dancing Dolphin, rose up the tunnel past the Worm, escaping on to the wide mountainside.

Whether it was the cold that drove him, or the singing that drew him, the Worm's tail slithered ever lower towards the cavern with its rushing river. At last it became impossible to avoid seeing it, coiled, spear-tipped in the glow of its own slime.

Kara shuddered. 'I'm not staying here with *that* for company. A princess does not care to sleep with serpents.'

They moved themselves deeper into the mountain, to the gravelly chamber at the foot of the steps. It was darker here, with a forlorn sense of being buried far from the daylight. The river plunged into its bottomless hole with a hollow sound of loss. The serpent's voice hissed round them with a new mockery.

'No one s-s-sees-s-s you now!'

'Poor thing,' said Mai. 'He must be very lonely.'

'Lonely!' Larsa scoffed, her eyes growing wide in amazement. 'Him? What about us?'

'We've got each other,' said Mai. 'Oh, I know. It's different for you. The princess and Elli and Oslaf are used to palaces full of servants and things. And you come from a big family. But I can hardly remember having anyone. I've always been alone. No! That's ungrateful. I had my geese.' She sniffed, but she was too late to stop two tears slipping out of her eyes as she thought of her brave, feathered friends. 'But here it's different. You can't imagine what it's meant to me. Oslaf's taught me to play knuckle-bones, you sing songs with us to cheer us up, Elli's shown me how to plait my hair, and the princess tells us, well, what it's like to be a king's daughter. But that old Worm, he hasn't got anybody to cheer him up, has he? All he ever says to anybody is "I s-s-see you". And even that isn't true.'

'He's got us,' chuckled Oslaf. 'We're his family.'

'Oh, don't!' Elli begged him. 'That's a horrible thought.'

'Oslaf,' Kara said sternly. 'You are a fool. A princess should not have to live in the company of idiots.'

That night Mai dreamed. She lay in the hollow she had scooped for herself in the cold, damp floor. In her dream there was warmth. A living, leaping heat like flames of fire. It played over her face, so that the clamped muscles relaxed into a smile. It breathed over her rasping throat, her cough-racked chest, her aching joints, and comforted them. With her eyes still shut she reached her arms up out of sleep and found a warm, hairy coat, a muscled neck, a throbbing pulse of life.

She woke with the memory of her smile still lingering. She stretched and yawned as though she had been in a soft feather bed, while the others shivered.

'Oh, I've had such a wonderful dream! I was warm, really warm, for the first time since the Raven took me out of the sun. You can't imagine what it was like.'

And she snuggled up against Larsa in her thin rags. Larsa gave a start and then hugged the younger girl close.

'You *are* warm! Like a little bonfire. How do you manage it?'

'Nonsense,' snapped Kara. 'You two are imagining things. Stupid peasants. How can a dream make anybody really warm?'

'I saw it,' whispered Elli. 'I saw your dream, Mai.'

'How could you?' asked Larsa sensibly. 'You can't see other people's dreams.'

'Am I always to be followed by idiots?' Kara scolded for the hundredth time. 'Is it not enough that Prince Oslaf talks like a fool? Must you copy him too?'

Only Mai knelt up and gazed at the other girl with a sort of hopeful longing.

'What was it, Elli? What did you see?'

'Something terribly big. Taller than a wolf, but white and furry, with a great arched back. It came bounding across the cave towards you. It frightened me, and yet I wanted to touch it, too. It licked your face and you put your arms round it.'

Mai stared into her wistful eyes. 'How did you know? I didn't tell you that! How can you possibly know what I dreamed?'

'I wish *I* could dream it. I'm so c-cold,' laughed Oslaf, and broke off in a spasm of coughing.

Larsa looked at him with concern.

'We've got to get out of here. Oh, I know, we've tried every tunnel. But there has to be a way somewhere. If we stay here much longer, we'll all grow ill and die.'

'I cannot think what my father, the king, is doing,' complained Kara. 'A princess does not expect to be kept waiting months to learn her fate.'

'It's all right for you,' Larsa said. 'Begging your pardon, your Highness. But all you have to do is say you'll marry Prince Oslaf, and you could be free tomorrow. You wouldn't be hurting anybody.'

She closed her ears to the princess's furious answer.

Mai's eyes were still following Elli as though she couldn't believe what the princess's maid had said. The prince wandered away to the brink of the hole down which the river disappeared. He leaned over. Not the faintest glimmer of gold came back from the rushing depths. Elli struggled to her feet and ran to catch him by the hand. He began to giggle.

'We haven't been everywhere, have we? We haven't been down there.'

Erc tried to ski faster. But his legs were unused to it, and already he was afraid of falling. Behind them the three dark points of menace were growing larger. Snow was flying from their paws. The wolves were like warships breasting white waves.

Pangur could not bear to watch them any longer. If he could see them, then soon they would be able to see him. He disappeared into the leather-smelling darkness.

Now it was worse. He could feel the straining of Erc's body and hear his laboured breathing as he tried to escape. But how could a boy outrun the wolves? And Pangur could only crouch and wait, not knowing at what moment the end would come.

He felt Erc twist round, throwing Pangur first one side and then the other. He must be looking over his shoulder to see how the wolves were gaining. Faster now for a few jerking strides. Then slowing gradually, as though unwilling to admit defeat even now. There was a jolting stop. Pangur could not stand it. He had to look out.

Three huge upturned muzzles, almost at Erc's shoulder height. Three sets of teeth lipped with moist black gums. Three pairs of eyes, red-sparked with anger.

Erc had thrown back his hood in response to a barked command.

'So!' snarled Harbard. 'A red-haired, freckled boy, just as the Sea-Wolves told us. I think we may have found our traitor.'

'And here . . . ' Ref walked round behind Erc and broke into a frenzied howl. 'It's him! The white cat! We have the two who set the Princess Finnglas free!'

For a petrified moment Pangur looked down, wide green eyes into red ones. He saw those eager, waiting jaws. Then, with the strength of terror, he leaped clean over the wolves' heads. He landed with a smack in the snow and struggled to find his feet. He was off, with awkward, ploughing leaps. The wolves plunged after him. But before the great paws and the questing mouths could reach him Pangur's claws were locked in the trunk of the nearest fir tree. He darted up it. Ref leaped into the air, almost twice his own height. Pangur's tail whisked through the wolf's teeth and out again, leaving a tuft of white hair as the wolf tumbled back. Ref howled with rage. The other two were running through the trees, looking up expectantly as Pangur raced along a branch and leaped to the next one, like a strange white squirrel.

Behind them Erc, still shaking, watched. Then, as if suddenly realizing what had happened, he started to ski away as fast as he could go. Thorvild and Harbard turned and saw him. With a roar they galloped in pursuit. On a high, horizontal branch Pangur arched his back and spat at Ref. Then he sprang on to the next tree. For a while Ref followed him, going ever further into the forest. The white gleam of the open road was fading behind them. There were millions of trees. A cat could hide for ever. Ref sat down in the snow and howled, this time in disappointment. Then he loped back after the others with his tail between his legs.

Pangur was alone. He walked delicately along a branch. The slender tip bent beneath him and its load of snow tumbled to the ground. Pangur leaped the next gap and picked his way to the tree-trunk. He curled up in the cleft and began to wash himself. The light was going. The trees creaked with cold. He was lost and friendless in the wastes of the Northlands.

'Arthmael!' he mewed. 'Arthmael?'

But how could the Dolphin reach him in the heart of the forest?

28

The wolves of the palace-guard were shepherding Bor across the courtyard to the dungeon-tower when Thorvild, Harbard and Ref came trotting through the gate with Erc between them. The young fisherman was drooping with weariness. The wolves waited impatiently while he released the unaccustomed skis from his feet. Bor watched, his eyes dark with horror. His face was almost as white as the snow that covered the yard.

As Erc stumbled nearer and raised his eyes in startled recognition, Bor cried out, 'I didn't tell them! Erc, you must believe me. I didn't betray you.'

Erc passed his hand over his eyes with a weary, puzzled smile.

'Of course you didn't, Bor. I never thought you had for a single moment. It was just bad luck. They must have spotted me as I went over the ridge. But we're not beaten yet. Pangur got away. Maybe he'll still be able to help them, even if we can't.'

'Help who?' Thorvild snarled behind him. 'What new treachery is this?'

Erc gasped and shut his lips in a terrified line.

'The dungeon,' snapped Harbard. 'They'll talk when the rats start to gnaw their toes.'

An old, scarred wolf nipped at Bor's heels.

'March, Bor, Witgan's son!'

Thorvild stopped short under the eaves of the hall.

'*Witgan!* Did you say Witgan's son? But it was Witgan's daughters who . . . '

A frenzied baying shook the town as they remembered Larsa.

'So, the plot unravels to its end. We have them almost all,' smiled Harbard. 'You thought to rescue her, did you? From the Serpent of Senargad? Fools! No one will come out of that prison until the Rhymester returns to undo the spell . . . if he ever does.'

They were almost at the tower door now.

'Keep them close,' Harbard ordered the scarred veteran. 'The Princess Finnglas and her bawling friend the monk will not dare to come back. So we have only to find the cat and two small children. If the king *does* return he will be well pleased with us.'

The door was creaking open.

'What can Pangur do?' hissed Bor. 'There's nobody left to help us now.'

As if in answer, there was a groaning overhead. A strange, stray breath of warm wind loosened the winter's weight of snow. It began to slither down the roof. The wolves gave a startled look up and leaped away. But Jarlath's great feasting hall was behind them. Here too the sliding snow was on the move. A white wet avalanche darkened the air and fell smothering on top of the boys and the wolves.

There was a stunned moment's silence. Bor struggled free. He saw a groping hand and hauled Erc out. Already wolves' tails were emerging, sharp ears, scrabbling paws.

'Run!' gasped Bor, dragging Erc with him.

'What's the good?' panted Erc, running all the same. 'They'll catch us before we reach the gate!'

'We're not going through the gate,' cried Bor, whiter than ever, but determined. 'Not that one, anyway.'

He was steering Erc across the courtyard at a stumbling run. The wolves were on their feet and leaping after them. A tall black shape reared in front of them, blocking their way. A standing stone. A granite hammer balanced against the darkening sky. The weapon stone of Thor.

Bor raced towards it, as though it was indeed a gate. As though he could follow where Kara and Elli and Oslaf had gone. As though the crack he saw could open and take them in.

110

And it did. Three steps leading down, and then darkness. The boys flung themselves into the hole. The stone clanged hollowly behind them. Outside the wolves scratched and howled in the wet, white world beyond return.

29

They had walked for hours. The tunnel seemed endless. The flecks of gold on the path only confused the boys' eyes in the darkness. There was a distant roar that they thought at first was the blood in their ears. It grew louder till it drowned the sound of their slow steps. But even without that fading echo they sensed that the walls were opening out and they could straighten up.

'Where are we?' whispered Bor, feeling for Erc. It was no use to pretend he was not afraid.

'How do I know?' said Erc, a little more sharply than necessary.

A floor of gritty sand. A scatter of tracks leading away in many directions into the shadows. That deep booming roar filling the air with a damp mist.

'We must remember the way back.'

Erc turned quickly. But already there were six tracks branching out behind them. They all looked alike.

'There is-s-s no way back,' a voice hissed from the walls around them.

Bor hid his face behind Erc, who was trembling also.

'You say you saw the princess come this way?' Erc asked.

'Yes, and her maid. And Prince Oslaf went running after them.'

'Then where are they now? Hallo-o-o!' he called.

A hundred hallos came back to him from the walls and the roof and the floor. But they were all his own voice.

'No one hears-s-s you.' The whisper held a savage satisfaction.

'We could try all these tracks. Only I'm so tired.' Bor sank down on the damp floor and rested his head on his knees.

Erc came and sat beside him. There was a hopelessness about this place that ate into the heart as the dank chill penetrated to the bone.

'If only Arthmael could be here!' he sighed. 'But he's far away now.'

Bor's voice came muffled. 'Erc. I've got to tell you. When I said I didn't betray you, it wasn't exactly true. I was on my way to the palace after I left you. The king had promised a chest of gold to anyone who would tell him who set Finnglas free. And ten chests of gold if the traitor was caught. And I was . . . Only I met the wolves before I got there. Then I saw the Dolphin. Arthmael. Dancing. I . . . he changed my mind. I didn't tell them, Erc. I never would have, after that. But I was going to.'

There was a moment's silence. Then Erc's arm came round Bor's shoulder and squeezed it.

'It's all right, Bor. You didn't do it. That's why you're in prison here with me now. But even if you had . . . All of us have done things we're ashamed of. I know I have. If we stopped being friends with each other because of that, everyone in the world would end up alone, wouldn't they?'

Bor gulped. 'You mean, you forgive me?'

'Bor!' Erc said. 'You silly! You're the only friend I've got now. I *need* you.'

Bor sat up straighter, as though a great weight had been lifted from him. Then he rose on to his knees and peered at the floor in front of them.

'Erc! Look! Can you see something? Footprints!'

Erc craned forward.

'I think you're right! There. Beside that track going downhill.'

'Let's follow them!' Bor scrambled to his feet.

'Careful. Don't tread on them.'

They had to bend almost double to see them. The floor shelved. The hollow booming was coming frighteningly nearer.

'There are lots of them. All muddled up.'

113

'Bor!' Erc stopped suddenly and peered closer. 'The princess was wearing shoes, I suppose. But what about her maid?'

'Of course she was. And Prince Oslaf had white boots.'

'But look. There's the print of a bare foot here in the sand.'

They looked at each other with a dawning hope.

'Could it be Larsa?'

They were hurrying faster now, with their eyes fixed on the trail. The tangled prints of several feet, some shod, some barefoot, criss-crossing at first, but then leading steadily down. A moment later Bor almost pitched over. He drew back in fright.

'Erc! There's nothing there! We've come to the edge.'

They could hear the river louder than ever, feel the spray as it flung itself down over the rocks. They could see nothing. Black as dreamless sleep. It seemed to have no ending. A single, terrifying plunge. The roaring in their ears went on and on.

'They couldn't have gone down there.'

'Look carefully,' ordered Erc. 'In every direction.'

The Worm-glow was very faint here. Its tracks kept away from the river. They checked the uncertain evidence of their eyes with cautious fingers.

'It is true,' said Erc unwillingly. 'Their footprints go to the edge and don't come back. All of them.'

'Then we should follow them.' Bor's voice sounded more doubtful than his words.

'But how?'

'Fools-s-s. Fools-s-s! *Fools-s-s!*' The serpent's hiss rose almost to a screech.

'Yes!' Erc shouted back at him. 'We *are* fools. What's wrong with that? So was Arthmael when he died for us.'

The long-drawn breath was like fat spattering on a fire. A sound of rage and pain.

But Erc was already on his knees at the chasm's edge, reaching down into the wet darkness. His hands found a narrow, slippery ledge.

'But we can't go down there,' Elli protested. She tried to drag Oslaf away from the hole, but he was too strong for her.

'Yes, I can.' He nodded vigorously. 'Watch me, Kara!'

'There *are* ledges,' said Larsa, leaning over and examining the rock face. 'But it's far too dangerous. I can't see to the bottom. There isn't a glimmer of light.'

'That means that the Worm has never been there,' declared Kara. 'So much the better. We shall go down. We cannot stay here any longer. A princess will not consent to be kept waiting six months for a hearing.'

'That's not what she said when she came,' murmured Larsa.

'People can change,' answered Mai.

'Oh, your Highness, no!' begged Elli. 'I can't! I really can't. It's pitch-dark down there. We'd fall to our deaths. We'll never get out again. Oh, please, you mustn't!'

'It's all right, Elli,' Mai said. 'You can stay here with me. I don't think it's the right way either. It's not that I'm afraid of climbing. I'm used to scrambling about on rocks. But I don't see how that can be the way out. We don't want to go down.'

'There is-s-s only one way out, and I am s-s-stopping it!' The hiss was triumphant.

But Oslaf sprang up at the sound. His face beamed with excitement.

'The Worm! The Worm's got the light. I'll go and get it!'

He dashed off up the steps beside the river at a lumbering run, before anyone could stop him.

'Oslaf! Where are you going? Come back!' Kara's order rang along the tunnel after him. But Oslaf's shadow had disappeared round the bend above.

115

'What is he doing? What's happening?' gasped Elli.

Kara sat down and tried to look composed.

'Don't fuss, Elli. The Worm is in the big cave below the tunnel-mouth now. Our brave prince will soon be back.'

They listened in silence.

'Poor Worm,' Mai sighed. 'I suppose we weren't very nice to him. Moving out as soon as he came to join us.'

'Nice!' exclaimed Larsa. 'Nice to *him*!'

There was a shout above. Then a terrible sound that began as a scream and ended in a roar. There were running footsteps. A gleam of light. Something heavy, slipping, tumbling down the steps. Oslaf pitched face forwards on the sand.

The prince lay in a pool of light that gilded his fair hair. One hand clutched his short sword, stained now. Outspread from the other, a glistening carpet flowed across the floor. Wide as a giant's cloak. Bright as hoarded gold. Wet as blood.

Larsa crept closer and stared down at it. The sparkling slime, already drying in the air. The pattern of huge scales.

'Dragon's skin!'

'Oh, Oslaf!' whispered Mai.

'I cut it from his tail,' shouted Oslaf, jumping to his feet. 'Look, Kara! I've got the light!' And he waved the sheet of dragon-skin in his hand.

'Oh, Oslaf! What have you done?' wept Elli. 'He will eat us all now!'

Kara whirled round on the others. 'How dare you criticize a prince! Has he not done what royal heroes should do?'

A bellow shook the cave. Louder than the falling river, louder than their hammering hearts. A huge head filled the top of the stairs. A vast body blotted out its own trail. He was pouring down the steps, howling horribly.

'Butchers-s-s! Cowards-s-s! Traitors-s-s! I s-s-shall des-s-stroy you!'

Now the light from Oslaf's trophy was playing on the questing face, the blinded eyes, the gaping mouth. There was no choice any more. They rushed to the brink of the waterfall. Oslaf was first. He tumbled over the edge, as though he had no fear, overjoyed at his success. The light from the skin, gripped between his teeth now, flashed on jagged juts and pinnacles of rock. Kara went after him, her skirt kilted up, like a warrior-queen following her standard-bearer.

'Oh, no, your Highness! Wait for me!' Terror and loyalty made Elli almost blind as she struggled to follow them.

Larsa kept beside her, her strong, capable hands guiding Elli's slippered feet from ledge to ledge, kindly but firmly unlocking Elli's fingers from frozen holds.

Mai came last of all, as though unwillingly. As her thin fingers let go of the floor and she dropped to the first ledge, she gasped, 'I'm sorry, Worm! Forgive us!'

But the baffled shriek above made even her heart quake.

There was a yell from below. A mighty splash. The light went out.

'Oslaf!' screamed Kara. 'You idiot! Where are you?'

The four girls clung to the rock in the darkness. Gradually they were aware of a growing radiance. Light glowed far underwater, showing the gleam of pebbles and the flicker of eel-like shadows. Slowly it rose, spreading itself across the surface, lighting now a vast black lake. The severed serpent-skin had stiffened, holding still the curve of the Worm's tail, like a hollow log that had been lined with gold. Oslaf was clinging on to one end of it, grinning up at them. He swam into the shallows and stood up, holding his boat proudly.

Kara stood on the last ledge. 'A princess does not paddle,' she said disdainfully.

Oslaf held out his arms. The princess hesitated a moment. Then she lowered herself into them.

'I bet he drops her,' hissed Larsa.

But he didn't. He set her gently in the boat, beaming with joy, and went back for Elli. Larsa tucked up her skirt and waded after them.

Only Mai stayed where she was. She was not afraid of the water. But she looked at the glistening skin with a kind of horror. Tears rolled down her scarred face and plopped into the lake.

'Come on,' urged Larsa. 'There's no going back.'

'Hurry up,' cried the Princess Kara. 'See! What we needed was the courage of princes, not the cowardice of peasants.'

Mai took Oslaf's hand and climbed sorrowfully aboard.

'Fools-s-s!' sobbed the Worm above them. 'You cannot es-s-scape!'

'We'll see about that!' said Larsa, dipping her hands into the water and starting to paddle.

'Oh, dear,' Elli quavered. 'What's going to happen to us? Which way shall we go?'

'We've no choice,' Larsa pointed out. 'We can't sail up that waterfall.'

And she steered them across the lake into the current.

The river took them. At first Larsa let the raft find its own course. They swam in a pool of gold of their own making, that made their faces glow and sparkled on the black surface of the water. Then as the walls drew threateningly close and the skin boat began to spin, Larsa borrowed Oslaf's sword and drove it through the water like a paddle. Threads of black blood and golden slime trailed past them as the sword was washed clean. With an effort Larsa kept the bow straight, blessing Erc's childhood lessons. Mai paddled as best she could with her hands, while Elli clutched the sides and Oslaf peered about him in a hopeful wonder. Kara sat regally upright in the middle of the boat as though it had all been ordered for her benefit.

A passage was opening before them. The river was dipping down a series of shallow weirs. The raft, laden with five people, was shipping water. Larsa, panting with exertion, called over her shoulder.

'Well, go on, your Highness, Elli, Oslaf! What are you waiting for? If you don't want us to sink, you'd better take off your shoes and start baling the water out.'

Mai stole a glance round, expecting the furious Kara to declaim what a princess would and would not do. But Kara, her mouth set in a rigid line, had already taken off her catskin slipper, sewn with amethysts, and was throwing water overboard with a calm efficiency. Elli scrabbled to do the same, but in her fright she scooped so fast that it was more like the flapping of a hen at the water's edge when her duckling brood first takes to the pond. Oslaf swung away with his boot, but he was looking around him too eagerly to do much good.

Between them they kept the craft level and moving in a straight line. It was impossible to tell where they were going. They sailed into darkness. Only the shining walls around them reflected their own passing light.

'Do you think,' said Elli, 'we shall ever come out to the sea? Or will it just empty into another lake in the middle of the mountain?'

No one answered her. It was too black a thought that the end of their voyagmie ght be to be buried deeper still.

'Listen,' said Larsa.

And 'Look!' called Mai at the same time.

There was the faintest lightening in the gloom before them. The least greying of the air that had been totally black. For the first time they could begin to make out what lay ahead. The river went on, swirling away into darkness. But the passage that carried it forked in front of them. A wide slope, like a road, came down to meet the water. And along this the light was dimly penetrating. It was so faint it was almost robbed of colour. But it had the grey honesty of daylight.

From the top of this tunnel came the distant howling of wolves.

31

They looked at each other as though this first glimpse of freedom was more frightening than the blackness of imprisonment. Then Kara stood up, threatening to sink the boat beneath them.

'Well. Is nobody going to move? Do we intend to escape or not?'

Oslaf started to follow her, making the raft rock wildly.

'Wait!' said Mai, more sharply than a goose-girl usually speaks to a princess. 'I don't think we're doing the right thing.'

The far howling of wolves reverberated down the tunnel. Larsa strove to hold the boat steady and tried desperately to think wisely for all of them. Into her mind came the shore where she had met Arthmael, the whistling grass and the long, bright sands. But it was hard to concentrate. The princess and Oslaf were already climbing out of the boat.

Mai bent over and closed her eyes. She was cold and wet and sick at heart. But in the stillness she began to feel that delicious warmth stealing over her again. Rubbing against her. Breathing on her face. Not daring to look, but more awake than dreaming this time, she hugged the hairy neck. She felt the heart beat against hers, strong, courageous. Then the muscled body broke her hold and growled.

Her eyes flew open. Oslaf and Kara were already on the shore, too impatient to wait. Elli was clambering forlornly after her mistress, clutching her wet skirt.

And the Hound was there, at the water's edge, facing her. A glorious white wolfhound. Immensely long legs and high arched back. All power and muscle and stilled speed. Its gums were drawn back terrifyingly over its teeth as it blocked the way, snarling.

Mai grabbed Larsa's sleeve. 'We must go back! We're doing something terribly wrong. Don't you see it?'

'See what?'

'The Hound! There! Right in front of us.'

'I can't see anything. But I can hear the wolves. They're coming closer.' Larsa was shivering uncontrollably.

But Elli cried out. 'Yes, Mai! I see it too. Oh, your Highness, come back at once!'

'Coward!' cried Kara. 'Shall I, the Princess of Senargad, be afraid of my father's Wolf-Guard? They would not dare to touch me. A princess does not know the meaning of fear.'

'Oh, please, your Highness. It's not the wolves I'm talking about, it's the Wolfhound. We must obey it.'

'Nonsense. I see no hound. You are day-dreaming. Since when was a servant wiser than a princess? You are a coward, Elli. Pull yourself together. What other way is there to freedom?'

Kara was starting up the passage as though she saw nothing between her and the daylight. The faithful Oslaf ran after her. Elli, weeping now, hurried to catch them.

Larsa tugged Mai's hand.

'Mai! Come on. I'm not sure we're doing the right thing, either, but . . . Mai! Your hand. It's warm again!' She stared down at the younger girl. 'I suppose it couldn't . . . But no, you've never met Arthmael, have you? He wouldn't have sent this to you and not to me. You'll have to come. We must keep together.'

Mai let herself be dragged ashore. As she stepped out, the Hound vanished from sight. The tunnel seemed darker than before.

'We should go back the way we came,' she whispered.

It sounded impossibly foolish. That way lay the Worm.

'We can't,' said Larsa.

Oslaf was in the lead now. Larsa had given him back his sword. He held it proudly drawn in front of him. Kara marched firmly behind him, her head held high.

121

The unhappy Elli kept close to her, shaking with fear and doubt but determined to stay loyal to her mistress, whatever happened. Larsa followed, uneasy too, though she could not say why. Mai trailed sorrowfully after them all.

The light was growing stronger all the time, though it lit only walls of rock. The air was warmer. Water was trickling down the sides of the path. They began to see each other clearly now. Faces eager, fearful, brave, miserable. The road was rising steeply.

But the sound of the wolves was sweeping nearer too. There came a space of silence, of imagined running. Then the baying broke out again close above them.

'Oh, please,' moaned Elli, catching at Kara's skirt. 'Let's turn back!'

'Let go, you baby! Have you no pride, no courage?'

They rounded a bend and for the first time in six months they saw the sky. Pale blue. Soft with spring sunshine. But something more startling loomed before it. Barring them from the light. Facing them with jaws open in a stern snarl. The white Wolfhound blocked the tunnel entrance. It growled at them to come no further.

This time they all saw it.

Kara strove to keep her voice natural.

'A royal beast, certainly. But not one I know from my father's kennels. Get down! Sit!'

The Hound growled alarmingly at her. The baying of the wolves was very loud.

'Please, your Highness,' begged Elli. 'Obey it. While there's still time.'

Kara rounded on her. 'Do you dare think I am afraid of Wolf or Hound? Obey! Have you forgotten I am a king's daughter?'

Elli shook her head dumbly. She leaned against the wall as though her feet refused to go on and defy the Wolfhound. Mai stopped beside her. But Kara moved forward with Oslaf, trying to make herself outstare the tall Hound. Outside the baying rose to a crescendo.

There was a flicker of movement between the Wolf-hound's legs. Something shot out and came tumbling towards them. Something small, something furry, something white as the Hound itself. Green eyes wide with terror. A little white cat went racing past them and disappeared down the tunnel the way they had come.

32

When Pangur woke in the fork of a tree he was wet. He looked up to see where the drips of water were coming from and a dollop of snow flopped in his face. He wiped it out of his eye and moved along the branch. All round him the forest was running with water. The boughs of trees were shedding their loads, springing upwards, the tops of bushes showed, already swelling with leaf-buds. The snow on the ground was turning greyer, translucent.

Pangur looked down in sudden panic. How had he got here? Would he ever be able to trace his way back to the road through the thawing snow? Would he be lost for ever in this vast forest, where every tree looked the same?

With a feeling of relief that made his legs go weak he spotted beneath him the tracks of the wolf. The prints were losing their shape as they melted, growing wider, as though something even more monstrous had passed this way while he slept. But he followed them steadily, leaping along the blackened bark of the wet branches.

It was a long journey. It did not seem possible that he could have run that far in his terror. But at last the forest gloom lightened and there was daylight ahead. He had found the road. He ran down the trunk of a tree and fell up to his neck in a heap of yielding snow. He floundered out and looked back. Of course. If he had run along the ground he could have seen the road long ago between the bare tree-trunks. But what is easy for a wolf is hard work for a cat with short legs.

A soft spring sunshine lit the length of the snowbound track. But the deep covering was melting as he watched. One moment crystals glittered like diamonds, the next they

124

had dissolved. Boulders were humping their heads out of the drifts. The sun sucked up a haze of moisture that hid the distant hills. Pangur sat down carefully and began to think. He was alone. At once a wave of longing swept over him. If only Arthmael were here to tell him what to do. But how could the loving Dolphin be on a forest road, far from the sea? It wasn't possible.

Behind him lay Senargad, and the captive Erc. Ahead lay unknown danger. There was no one to help him now if he went on. It seemed an easy choice. But his chin went up. He was no ordinary cat. He was Pangur Bán. He had promised Finnglas that he would go for her and rescue those who were in prison for her sake. Erc was captured. There was no help for that. Pangur was the only one left now who could free Larsa and Mai. But where? And how?

'Oh, Arthmael,' he sighed. 'I wish I'd asked your help when I still had the chance.'

Then, shaking off the snow with a twitch of his tail, he began to walk.

The miles rolled behind him. Up hill and down, but mostly up. The snow was giving way to grey puddles, brown earth and yellowed grass. He was wet with melting ice and spattered with mud and very tired.

He came over a ridge. Ahead of him mountains rose dramatically, clad in black fir-forests, their peaks still glittering with snow. But the quiet, lonely world was horribly changed. In the valley below him a battle was raging by a river-ford. The shocking sound of it rose clearly on the still spring air. The clash of steel. The screams of falling men and horses. The ravenous howling of wolves and roaring of bears. The armies were locked together, the golden standard of Senargad against the ice-blue of Bergenring. And over it all, like a thundercloud, hung a gigantic raven, darkening the ground with her wings. Every few moments she swooped down upon the battlefield and seized another victim, gorging herself with shrieks of greed.

Pangur shuddered. Spring had woken more than the flower-buds. Jarlath and Thidrandi had returned to their war.

The road made straight for the ford and the thick of the battle. He could not go that way. Besides, quite apart from the fighting, he was not sure that he wanted to cross that ford. One more valley, one more river, and then a strange land. Had he come too far? Uncertain now, he began to make a wide circle towards the head of the dale.

Now Pangur found himself not avoiding snowdrifts but seeking them out. Letting his white body glide in front of them unseen. He was dropping lower. The grey wave of the Wolf-Guard was thinner now, still launching themselves furiously against Thidrandi's men. They hurled themselves high into the air, trying to strike between the helmets and the shining coats of dwarf-mail. Behind them, Jarlath's spearmen were few and scattered. Many bodies lay strewn in the trampled mud. Was Bor's father there among the fallen? Or was he still thrusting his spear with a weary arm?

But Thidrandi's side were falling back too. Now they were desperately defending the borders of their kingdom. There was no sign of the huge black bear that legend had said marched at the head of Bergenring's army.

At the back of the battlefield a solitary tent had been pitched. It was hung with strange skins, and feathers, and bleached skulls. Its door opened into shadow.

Fire streaked from that tent doorway. Pangur gasped. Jarlath's sword flashed in the air again. As if powered by shafts of lightning the wolves flung themselves into the fray with doubled fury. Bergenring's army wavered. Warriors were stumbling back across the river. But at the water's brink the pursuing wolves halted suddenly. Their large paws braked violently in the mud. They howled as though in terror of the water. Again power shot from the Rhymester's tent. One black wolf leaped high into the air as though he would fling himself to the further bank. Arched over mid-stream he began to fall, twisted, howled, and dropped into the rising water. It should not have been deep enough to drown him, but his body was swept downstream, as stiff and lifeless as a broken tree.

126

With a cry of desolation the other wolves turned, tails lowered between their legs. They began to flow uphill, beside the river, as though searching for some place where they might cross dry-footed.

Pangur watched it all with a fascinated horror. He sat perched on the hillside, like a pocket of unmelted snow. The wolves were sweeping nearer. He could see the red fury of their eyes now, as once he had seen them turn on him in Jarlath's palace.

'Yee-ow!'

He woke to the sudden terror of the present. He was not just a spectator, sitting beside the river watching the battle and wondering which way to go. He was right in the path of the charging Wolf-Guard. He, the white cat, who had set the Princess Finnglas free!

Almost too late, he turned and fled. He knew from the baying that shook the mountain that they had seen him. He twisted and doubled, between the rocks, racing for his life. But how could his tiny legs outrun the leaping wolves? No trees this time to shelter him. No hiding-place. No friends.

'Arthmael!' his breath sobbed.

Far, far away the wide tossing ocean, the dancing Dolphin's home.

There was something on the skyline. Pangur almost fainted with fright. He tried to dodge aside, but it moved easily ahead of him. A single commanding bark rang down the hill.

He glanced fearfully at it. An immensely tall, lean, snow-white wolfhound. It could have eaten him up with one snap of its long jaws. He twisted round and dashed for the river. But terrifyingly the Hound was there before him, standing at the edge of the trees.

Pangur threw a look over his shoulder. The pack was gaining rapidly. Wolves behind him. The Wolfhound still running on his left. He bounded up the ridge. For a moment he thought he had lost the dog. But a desperate look showed it waiting for him on the crest. With a gasp he turned to his right, galloping as hard as he could on four short legs, straining diagonally to reach a dip in the skyline. He tumbled over a ledge of rock and went skidding downhill.

The wolves' baying broke out again as they breasted the ridge and saw their quarry. There was no time to look back. He could only imagine them surging after him down the hill like an advancing tide. But a swift glance left met the white Hound flowing closer beside him. How soon before it overtook his short strides? How long could one cat hold out against a great dog and an army of wolves? He almost stumbled in his despair.

He did not see the Hound turn back, doubling between Pangur and the oncoming wolves. He hardly heard the urgent bark to him to go on. A few more bounds. A mouth opened before him in a low cliff face. A wide stone passage leading down into the mountain. At the last moment the Wolfhound sprang past Pangur and turned at bay in the tunnel entrance. Its loud ringing bark challenged the oncoming wolves. Running too fast to stop, the terrified Pangur streaked through its legs into the down-rushing darkness.

33

The Hound stood magnificent in the entrance, barking more urgently than ever. In front of Elli and Mai, Larsa stopped too. She was afraid of this huge, stern, snow-white beast. Yet it was not just fear that forbade her to disobey it. She felt a sudden, loving hope. Could Arthmael's spirit really be here, even in this dire danger? But Kara strode on, and Oslaf would not leave her.

Behind the Hound the wolves swept into sight round the rocks. The bright world beyond the cave was lost in a fighting, snarling mass of bodies. The Wolfhound sprang round, heroically at bay. Solitary, splendid, it faced the Rhymester's horde. For a moment the wolves cowered back, daunted by its unyielding courage. Then they launched themselves into a frenzied attack. It was horrible to see. The lone white Hound besieged by grey, brindled, black snapping jaws. Firm shoulders rising out of a sea of lunging bodies. All that speed and grace imprisoned within two walls of rock. Blood flew, and hair, and spittle.

Not one step back did the Wolfhound give. Its growl rose. It pleaded as well as menaced, as though even now the Rhymester's tide of hate could be turned. But the wolves, impatient with anger, saw their chance and seized it. The passage was too wide, the Hound alone. Even Kara and Oslaf had halted in dismay. Braggi, captain of the Wolf-Guard, bounded past the Hound and all the pack poured after him. As the Hound's command rang out yearningly to stop them one or two of them faltered and looked back, but the rest were deafened, maddened.

Bergenring's prince stood with his sword held valiantly in front of him. A vague smile still lingered on his worried face.

129

Kara hesitated for a moment. But fight was impossible. As Oslaf's first cuts brought a howl from the leading wolf the princess grabbed his hand and fled. There was no talk of the courage of princesses now.

Mai was already running, with Larsa after her. Kara's long legs soon overtook them. In the rear Oslaf kept turning and hacking at their pursuers, winning time for the others to escape. As they turned the corner into shadow the Hound broke through the wolves and stood at bay again, protecting their flight. Blood streaked its white coat from many wounds. This time another figure stood beside it, closing the gap. Elli.

Ahead of the running prisoners the thick darkness was lit again by a glow of gold. Their raft of serpent-skin, dark-green outside and glistening within, lay half in and half out of the river, where they had left it. In the middle, back arched, ears flattened, tail erect, was the white cat.

There was no time for questions. They tumbled aboard. Oslaf was nursing a gash from Braggi's teeth. Mai pushed them out, edging the laden boat through the quiet backwater towards the fork where the river rushed on downwards. Suddenly Larsa cried out, 'Elli! Where's Elli?'

Kara rose. Her head almost touched the tunnel roof. She gripped the rock, staring back up the passage down which they had fled.

'Elli!' she screamed. 'Elli! Where are you?'

The tunnel was a confusion of leaping shadows. The glimmer of the Wolfhound beset by raging wolves. And by his side, blocking the other half of the passage, stood Elli. Weaponless, with only the soft flesh of her body as a barrier, she guarded her royal mistress's road to escape.

'The idiot! I must go back!' Kara's voice hissed like the serpent's. Still she did not seem able to move.

The wolves surged forward on the defenders, like dark storm-waves at night.

Oslaf was stumbling to his feet too. He pitched out of the boat on to his knees in the water. Larsa, as white as the princess, grabbed at him.

'It's too late, your Highness.'

The faint gold light of the boat showed Elli falling before the rushing pack, like a willow-branch in a flood. It lit briefly the wide gash that was staining her white blouse black. The mass of wolves blocked out the crueller daylight, that would have shown her life-blood in its true colour.

The prisoners in the water stayed still and stricken.

There was no holding the wolves now the gap was open. Baying victoriously they surged on down the tunnel like a river in spate.

'Elli! She died to save me!' whispered Kara, shocked beyond belief. 'Little, timid Elli, that I mocked for a coward?'

Larsa and Mai, weeping but practical, were pushing the boat out into the current. As the red eyes of the wolves swept nearer they dragged Oslaf aboard.

'Sit down, your Highness,' ordered Larsa. 'We're not safe yet.'

'I must rescue her body,' Kara cried. 'For honour's sake. Even if I were to die in the attempt.'

'You can't,' said Larsa. 'There are a hundred wolves between us and her.'

'But I laughed at her! And yet she has done what only a princess does to save her people.'

'Then take the last gift of life she has given you. Don't throw it away now.'

'I can't leave her to the wolves!'

'The wolves will not have her. Look!' gasped Mai.

The pack had stormed to the brink of the river. They checked there, howling dismally, as though the Rhymester's enchantment faltered before the touch of running water. The boat was no more than three strides away, but not one of them would risk so much as wetting a large paw.

But it was not at them that Mai was staring in wonder. Further back, where the tunnel sloped up towards the day, the Wolfhound was bending over the tumbled body of Elli. First it licked her wounds, tenderly, caressingly, cleansing her. Then it lifted its pointed muzzle and from its throat broke a sound they had never heard from it before. An eager, joyous yapping, like a young dog let loose from its chain.

131

And round the two of them a light began to grow that was not the Worm-trail nor the common daylight. It was glowing, many-coloured, painting the rock with every hue from scarlet to violet. At its touch the walls of the tunnel were splitting open to a vast blue sky. Arched from the cave, from the deep place of death high into the heavens, sprang a bridge in all the banded colours of the rainbow.

The white Hound lowered its head again. Very gently, as if she weighed no more than a feather, it lifted Elli in its jaws and began to pace on to the rainbow bridge. Slowly at first, then with long, leaping, springing bounds, carrying her up into the dazzle of the sun.

Their eyes were pricking with unbearable light. They did not know the moment at which the two were lost in glory. The current spun the boat violently round. Hound, passage, wolves were all gone, and they were back in swirling darkness, with Pangur as passenger in place of Elli.

After a while the white cat sat upright, still trembling. Yet he raised his chin and looked boldly at the princess.

'King Jarlath's daughter, I presume?'

The guilt-stricken Kara could not speak. But Larsa lifted the cat on to her knee and fondled his ears.

'The white cat himself! You must be Pangur Bán. You're a friend of Erc, aren't you?' And her face, that had long since lost its tan, blushed deep in the shadows.

'Then you're Larsa! And you must be Mai. Thanks be to Arthmael! I thought I'd never find you.' And Pangur broke out into loud purring and rubbed his head under her chin.

The current carried them on. Presently Oslaf laughed.

'Fast! Going faster.'

Larsa stiffened and sat up.

'It's more than that. The water's rising.'

The roof was sweeping lower. Waves were building up as the press of water fought its way between the rocks.

'The snow!' cried Mai. 'It must all be melting at once. It's going to flood the tunnel.'

They crouched lower. There was no stopping the raft. Larsa gripped Mai's hand.

132

Oslaf's head struck the rock above. He flung up his arm to shield it. The raft hung wedged between the roof and the water. The current tore at it, trying to drag it on. They were being sucked under. Pangur clung to Larsa. The pot-girl tried to smile at them all.

'Courage!' she said. 'Remember Elli. Let us die as bravely as she did. But if only I could have known what happened to Hygd and Sigi.'

The river rose higher. Mai dipped her hand in the gold-lit water rushing past them.

'I wish this was the salt sea. I've never seen it. I wish I could have met Arthmael just once and talked to him, like you two have. But now I never shall.'

Larsa's hand covered hers as she looked back up the black tunnel. 'Mai!' she said. 'I think perhaps you have already hugged him.'

The roof pressed lower.

'Isn't there something we can try?' begged Larsa. 'You know Arthmael better than any of us, Pangur. What would he want us to do?'

'In a fix like this there is only one thing left to do,' gasped Pangur. 'Sing!'

'Sing?' choked Kara. 'Now?'

But Larsa's eyes met Pangur's bravely, and her voice rose with his.

> 'No prison can crush us,
> And death cannot hold us.
> The love of the Dolphin
> Will always enfold us.'

34

And what of Sigi and Hygd?

As the barnacle geese came drifting down in the autumn evening, Brodd and Odd raised their wings in greeting. But while the wild geese and the farm geese talked together, something else was greying the surface of the lake. Ice was beginning to form around its margins.

'You should come south with us.'

'Stupid to stay here.'

'The cold will get you.'

'Bergenring is no place to stay the winter.'

'And this will be the bitterest winter of all.'

'Go south with us. Soar over the sea to the Summer Land.'

'I wish we could,' Brodd clucked sadly. 'But we couldn't possibly fly that far. Odd was exhausted just with the journey from Senargad.'

She spoke fondly, with a little wifely pride that her grey wings had outlasted his.

'At least get the children to shelter before the snow comes. Will you try there?'

And they all twisted their long necks to stare at the castle on its island with their strange golden eyes.

'I don't know. There's nowhere else that I can see.'

'Do you know who lives there?' asked Odd.

The water rippled as they preened their feathers, settling themselves more comfortably for sleep.

'They say it is the Queen of Bergenring's castle.'

'But we do not know who keeps it.'

'No one ever comes out.'

When the children woke, chilled and stiff in the morning, the wild geese had already flown.

'*We* could have gone with them,' said Hygd, too late. Then, throwing her arms round Brodd's neck, 'But we wouldn't leave you alone!'

'There, there. That's as may be,' said Brodd. 'Now what's to be done?'

'Best be careful,' warned Odd. 'Bergenring is an old friend of Senargad. They say the prince and princess are to be married one day.'

'All the same. The queen wouldn't turn two children away, would she? Even if she is there.'

'Who's to say? It's four walls and a roof. That's what humans need. Wait there.'

He paddled off, disappeared around the island and finally came into sight on the other side, swimming towards them between the shore and the castle, under the raised drawbridge.

'Silent as the grave,' he reported. 'And about as friendly.'

'Oh, don't be silly,' scolded Brodd. 'If there's nobody at home, we might as well make use of it as wait till we freeze to death. Perhaps they only come in the summer.'

The children climbed aboard once more and Odd and Brodd sailed out from the shore. They paddled slowly and awkwardly. They were no more used to swimming than flying.

The castle floated nearer. Steep wooden walls of overlapping shingles. Carved bears' heads on the gable ends. And round one corner a single, narrow stone tower. It seemed to be rooted in the boulders at its base.

The geese were swimming in shadow now. The water was dark and very deep. The mountains seemed to rush straight into the water, down, down, down, as though they would never stop. Hygd clutched Brodd's warm feathers more tightly. Odd glided in between the boulders beneath the tower.

'This is as good as anywhere,' he hissed very low. 'I shouldn't think anyone has seen you.'

The children scrambled ashore. The two geese shook the water from their wings and waddled after them.

There were wide windows in the wooden walls, dark slits in the stone tower. Blank, eyeless, they stared across the water as though unaware of what was coming to trouble their silence.

'Where's the door?' whispered Hygd.

Sigi said nothing, but led the way around the tower. It was there, as he had been sure it would be. A low stone arch, a heavy studded door. An iron handle. Somehow he knew it would open. And it did. The latch clanked. The hinge creaked. No one called or came.

Nine steps led down, and then the stairs began to climb again, circling around the walls of the tower. Sigi went first. He had to stoop his head, though he was not yet fully grown. Hygd, wide-eyed, was behind him, and the geese flapping and panting in the rear.

An empty room, overlooking the lake. A low, bare table. High-backed carved chairs. Dust.

Another room above. A bed with faded hangings. The cobwebbed curtains once richly-embroidered.

A third turn of the stairs. A light clink of metal. The first sound in the castle, stopping their hearts for a moment and their feet for longer.

A half-open door. A startled figure jumping from his stool to the floor and sweeping all the contents of his bench into his leather apron. A little man, no bigger than Hygd, with red-brown beard tumbling over his chest and a red knitted cap. But he had been too quick. Almost all his work was bundled out of sight. But one piece fell, among the snips and shavings of metal on the floor. It lay between them, glittering wickedly in the light from the water. A magnificent necklace of rubies and diamonds.

35

The little man had bright, dark eyes, like a bird's darting to and fro in search of food. But it was not food that he was hungry for. These eyes flew to the jewels in the dust. To Hygd and Sigi's faces in the doorway. All round the cluttered workroom. With an expression of fear and alarm he clutched his apron to his chest like a bag. There could be no doubting what it must hold.

Hygd took a step into the room, hardly knowing what she was doing. Her eyes grew wider and wider as she stared at the precious necklace, at the rubies, the diamonds, the intricate pattern of gold that wove them together. The children had never seen anything like it in their short lives, not even when King Jarlath and Princess Kara rode through the city. The dwarf's look flicked back to hers. A quick, cunning smile flashed across his face and was hidden again. His bushy brows shot up towards his hair.

'Out! Out!' he shouted, running towards them, and slammed the door.

They heard him scampering round the room, the rattle of pots, the scrape of furniture, the slamming of lids. The door was snatched open and his face appeared again, grinning broadly.

'Come in! Come in!' He swept off his cap and bowed low, chuckling as he did so. Not knowing what else to do, they obeyed him nervously, tiptoeing into the room and staring round at it. Odd waddled in, but Brodd stayed suspiciously in the doorway.

Whatever the dwarf had hidden in his apron had vanished. The leather garment hung down to his knees. His workbench was tidy, with jeweller's tools laid out in neat

137

rows. There were shelves stacked high to the ceiling with flasks and jars and pouches, and a step-ladder beside them. Round the floor were many carved chests. In the corner a furnace winked. And in the centre of the bench, brighter than the sparkle of the lake through the window, lay the ruby necklace.

The dwarf bent over it. He murmured to it, stroked it, lifted it, cradled it. His glance shot back to the children with startling swiftness. Questions rapped out.

'Who are you? How did you get here? Where do you come from?'

Hygd and Sigi looked at each other, seeking for advice. Sigi answered.

'We come from Senargad. We had to run from some wolves. We came here to escape them.'

'Running from wolves, eh? Then you're no friends of King Jarlath. So what is to be done with you till the king and queen return?'

His eyes searched their faces shrewdly, as if he saw more than Sigi had said. Then slowly he held up the necklace in his cupped hands. He was offering it to Hygd. Holding it under her chin. The glow of its jewels played over her skin. The little girl stood spellbound, not daring to believe what was happening. The dwarf's brown, wrinkled hands came round her neck, drawing the ends of the fox-headed clasp together. The necklace fell, cool and heavy, against the base of her throat. Hygd put up a wondering hand to touch it, as if she still could not accept that it was real.

Sigi stared, struggling to understand why the dwarf should do this. The goldsmith gave a short bark of laughter.

'Ha! A little present from Grinni. Wear it to remember me.' Then he whispered deep in his beard, ' . . . and to forget much else.'

He turned abruptly and seemed to see the two grey geese for the first time. He darted at them, waving his arms and shouting, 'Geese! Here! I never heard of such a thing. Out! Shoo!'

He aimed a kick at Odd, who stumbled backwards into Brodd, and the two went tumbling down the stairs in a flurry of squawking. The door slammed again. Outside there was a furious hissing. Brodd's beak hammered on the door.

'Whatever next? Come out! We'll see about this!'

But the door stayed shut. The dwarf jumped up and down in frenzied glee. Sigi ran at him.

'How dare you! How dare you kick Odd like that? Those geese are our friends. They flew us away from the wolves. Let them in, do you hear me?'

The dwarf chuckled till he had to clutch his sides.

But Hygd said nothing, saw nothing. She stood before the window, looking down and stroking her beautiful necklace over and over again.

Sigi raised his hand, as though uncertain whether to strike Grinni. But the dwarf seized his hand and ran with him to the side of the room. He stopped before a richly-carved chest. It was hinged with iron and patterned with bears and swans and serpents. Grinni lifted the lid, watching Sigi's face as he did so and laughing to himself.

He had calculated well. Sigi could not restrain a gasp of wonder. The dwarf reached into the chest lovingly. Strong fingers slipped beneath the links of gold. He drew his treasure out carefully, swinging, swaying, glittering in its shimmer of close-knit chains. He held it up against Sigi's chest, as though measuring it for size. A corselet of golden chain-mail, fit for a prince to wear. And Sigi's hand, like Hygd's, strayed upwards as though drawn by a magnet and caressed its magical metalwork.

'Put it on,' urged the dwarf.

And Sigi slipped it over his head. He stood up, and the dwarf-armour settled snugly round his body.

There was a long silence in the tower room. Grinni's glinting eyes watched his two visitors and his smile widened, mocking them.

'A true prince and princess!'

On the other side of the door the scolding died to a worried gobble. Presently two geese went swimming sadly

139

past the tower. Sigi and Hygd did not even look up to see them go.

Grinni gave his sudden laugh again and rubbed his hands.

'Well! We have a royal bed below, though it's not been slept in these many years. And there's plenty of food in the kitchen.'

He threw open the door and bellowed down the stairs.

'Grid! Come up, my precious! We have guests at last.'

36

'How can we climb down there in the dark?' asked Bor, drawing back from the edge of the chasm.

'It's not completely dark. Look. There are traces of gold on the rocks.'

Bor forced himself to look over. It made him dizzy. The bottomless dark, with just the faintest glitter of gold. The ceaseless crashing of the waterfall. The echoing walls.

'But what if we do get down? What's the point? Listen to the water.'

'*They* went down. And they haven't come back.'

Erc's voice trailed away. He had meant it to be a statement of faith and hope. But even he could see a colder meaning to his words.

'Bor, I'm sorry. But if they *did* go this way, then so must we. We have to follow them.'

Bor gulped. 'All right,' he said. He made the words sound careless, as though it was no more than deciding which way to go for an evening stroll.

Erc went first, with the skill of one used to clambering over wet rocks and collecting gulls' eggs.

'You can't see much when you're climbing down anyway,' he panted. 'It's mostly a matter of feeling for the next toe-hold.'

'Ouch!' gasped Bor.

'What's up?'

'Something hit me in the face.'

'A falling stone? Watch out. Though it should be me that catches it on the head.'

'No, it wasn't a stone. It was water . . . Erc! It's pouring over the edge.'

'It can't be. We're well clear of the waterfall. And the cave floor was . . . well, not dry . . . but it wasn't running with water.'

'Well, it is now. Help! I'm soaking wet.'

He knew from Erc's intake of breath that the cold sluice of water had hit him too. Erc looked up in alarm.

'Listen!'

The steady boom of the waterfall was rising to a roar. They began to glimpse the foam as it hit the river below surging up to meet them. Moment by moment the golden trail down the rocks was growing shorter.

'Bor! The water's rising. The river is in flood!'

'What do we do?' The boy's voice was high with panic.

'Up!' ordered Erc. 'Get back on top before it sweeps us away.'

They were scrambling up a lesser waterfall. The walls were running with the new deluge that tried to pluck their hands from their holds and make their feet slip. Thankful for one danger past they hauled themselves back up to the cave and met another.

Water was swirling over the floor. The sandy gravel underfoot was on the move. They heard the spate splashing down the steps. And with every spreading wave it was blotting out the trails of light, filling the tunnels with a wet, icy darkness.

'Quick,' said Bor. 'Back up one of those passages that lead higher than this.'

They started across the cave but quickly checked. Every tunnel was a river now. Water poured at them from all directions. It was rising round their knees.

'S-s-stop! S-s-stop!' shrieked the serpent's voice.

It was too dark to see him coming, but they smelt the air turn foul. They heard a brushing, clawing, thumping, as though something huge was being swept down the stairs.

'Ah! S-s-stop! My s-s-skin! My tail!'

The wounded Worm threshed in the water, sending colossal waves over the two boys. They backed away, clinging together. The water was up to their waists.

'Es-s-scape! There mus-s-st be es-s-scape,' sobbed the Worm. 'Oh, pleas-s-se, s-s-stop!'

They heard a mighty splashing as he struggled against the tide. Then a scrabbling, the dry scrape of claws, a long-drawn hiss of pain. The washing of the waves died away. But the slow slithering went on above the river's rush.

'What's happening? Where is he?' whispered Bor.

'He's taken the only way left,' Erc muttered. 'Up.'

A golden light was growing on the wall, painting it with radiance, like a cloth of gold. Over it, like black smoke writhing, the vast shadow of the Worm was crawling painfully. His tail hung down, like a dark rent in the backcloth of his shining slime. It dragged heavily. From it dripped thick, black blood. With each upward jerk the Worm let out a hissing moan.

'Oh, s-s-stop! My s-s-skin. S-s-stop.'

The flood had reached their chests now. They could hardly stand.

'What are we going to do?' Bor was shouting at Erc.

The spreading glow showed a wall of water roaring down the upper stairs towards them. Erc plunged after the Worm.

'What choice have we got?' he cried. 'Follow him!'

Part 3

37

Niall was at his morning prayers on the Summer Isle.
The Irish monk did not sit, or kneel, or even stand in the
chapel with his hands lifted to heaven. No, he had waded
out into the periwinkle waters of the bay below Finnglas's
half-restored palace. He wore a new white wool gown, and
though he had tucked it up into his knotted girdle, the hem of
it was patterned with green eel-grass and silver-grey sand as
though it had been embroidered. He was singing his prayers
and praises at the top of his lusty voice, to the astonishment
of the local fisher-folk and the passing seagulls.

> 'Thou who guidest Noah over the flood
> waves,
> Hear us!
> Who with thy word recalled Jonah from
> the abyss,
> Deliver us!
> Who stretched forth thy hand to Peter as
> he sank,
> Help us! . . . '

'Very appropriate, in the circumstances.'

A blunt, blue-black head with a white chin rose out
of the water, level with his. Small, bright eyes stared at
him.

'What the . . . ? Oh, it's you, Arthmael. That's funny, I
was just calling on you.'

'What's funny about that? I heard you. So, I imagine, did
every fishing boat from here to Brittany. As it happens, I was
coming anyway. I need your help urgently.'

'Of course . . . No, wait a moment. I thought I was asking *you* for help.'

'Did you now? Ah, well, prayer is full of strange surprises. Would you mind running up the hill to fetch Finnglas? There's not much time.'

'I'm not sure about Finnglas. They've just finished a week of feasting and games for her coronation. All the kings and queens and chieftains and nobles from every tribe you ever heard of, and then more besides. They're going home today. And Finnglas plans to ride part of the way with them.'

'*I'm* sure about Finnglas. Hurry, man. That's her, in the green gown with her arms round Cloud-Clearer. Quick, before she's into the saddle and away.' The Dolphin was jumping up and down with impatience, making a great deal of splashing.

Niall caught his urgency. He floundered out of the water and ran barefoot up the hill as fast as he could.

A great, colourful crowd had gathered outside the gates of Rath Daran. Fine horses tossed their heads, making their harness dance in the light of the sun. Horsemen bucked and pranced and snorted, as high-spirited as the mounts they rode. There were chariots full of fair and laughing women. Parade-weapons and armour flashed with many jewels, and there was gold in braided hair and around smooth white necks. All were going home heavier with riches from Finnglas's treasure.

In the centre of them all was Finnglas, in the gay green gown of Maytime, with hawthorn flowers in her hair. The throng gave way to let Niall through as respectfully now as if the young monk had been a druid of old.

He muttered in Finnglas's ear. 'Arthmael is here. He needs you at once.'

She flashed a merry smile round her guests.

'Excuse me a moment. I shall be back before the wine-cup has finished going round.'

Then she ran down the hill beside Niall, with her skirts held up to her knees like a young girl.

Arthmael greeted her fondly.

148

'I'm sorry, Finnglas. I gave you as long as I could. But the need is urgent.'

'Erc! Pangur! They have failed? They're in danger?'

Arthmael swayed his head from side to side. 'Yes and no. They have been . . . how shall I put it? . . . a little rash, and a little unlucky. Pangur, at least, has found the prisoners. They have not failed yet, but they are indeed in danger. Will you come?'

Finnglas's eyes flashed with eagerness. 'Of course I will come! It almost broke my heart to watch them fly away while I was left behind in safety. Oh, for the feel of a sword in my hand again!'

'Finnglas! It may not be by the sword that this battle is won.'

'What do you mean? I don't understand you.'

'Yet, without understanding, you will come, brave heart?'

'You know I will. Only . . . '

'Yes?'

'How can I get across the North Sea so quickly?'

His eyes twinkled at her.

'Was it for nothing they called you Finnglas of the Horses?'

Niall looked puzzled. But a slow smile of wonder grew on Finnglas's face.

'So be it!'

She ran back up the hill to her waiting guests, arriving flushed and bright-eyed.

'Forgive me, friends! All you who came to share in my rejoicing. The hand of God guide your horses and the speed of the Spirit fill your sails. But Finnglas must ride another road today. I take the first adventure of my reign. Go now in joy, and may the bond of peace between us never be broken . . . Cousin Rohan, will you ride out along the way with our noble guests, and do them honour in my place?'

The horses were given their heads. The chariots bucked and bounded forward over the roads. There was cheering and waving on every side. Some guests only trotted down to the

149

harbour and boarded there the tall-sailed ships. Others set off with a flourish for the far mountains and coasts across the Summer Land.

Finnglas put her arms round her chestnut stallion and kissed his velvety nose.

'Will you forgive me too, Cloud-Clearer? If only I could take you with me. But I must ride a stranger steed than you today. Wait for me.'

The horse rubbed her cheek in understanding.

The nobles of her court were still standing round her, tugging their moustaches in doubt and surprise. Finnglas beckoned to three of them.

'Tomméné. Manach. Laidcenn.'

She led them up to a grassy knoll in full view of everyone and made them stand around her. Then she joined their hands to hers, over the queen's sword. Tomméné mac Ruain, her master of horses. Her uncle Manach, leader of her hosts. Laidcenn, prince of the bards.

'So. Receive power from me, until I come again. Carry it nobly. I had not thought to leave you so soon.'

'Then take us with you,' interrupted Tomméné. 'Our queen should have horsemen, swords, warriors. She should not adventure alone, like a wandering minstrel.'

'I must go with speed. And where I ride, you cannot follow. I have other guardians that you do not know of. I need you here, Tomméné. I leave a land at peace with itself and with its neighbours. But it needs good counsel. In this handclasp I hold the wisdom of friends and family. Swear now that you three will guard the Summer Land and keep the queen's peace until I return.'

Old Manach, captain of warriors, looked curiously at the others. But their faces showed only faith and loyalty. He joined his voice to theirs, loudly, in the presence of the people.

'We do so swear to serve the queen.'

And all the people shouted, 'We hear you!'

Finnglas reached up and kissed them each farewell. Then she was off, like a swallow skimming over the grass.

Almost at once she was down on the beach again. The rich gown had gone. She was dressed, as if for riding, in a red tunic and soft buckskin trousers. Niall was ready too, with a leather satchel on his back and a stout staff in his hand. But he still looked puzzled. There was no sign of Arthmael.

'I suppose you understood how we're getting there?' he asked. 'I'm not sure I did.'

Finnglas put her fingers to her lips and whistled, shrill and clear.

The wind began to rise. Long rollers of emerald green came racing into the bay, topped with a crest of creamy foam. The waves began to break around their feet, tugging at the very stones they stood on. Finnglas cupped her hands to her mouth and shouted across the gale.

'Manannan! Manawydan! Son of Lir!'

From the tallest of the waves a voice neighed back to her.

'Who calls the wild sea-horses?'

'For the love of the wind, and the joy of the running waves, Finnglas of the Horses gives you greeting.'

'We serve no one. We will not stay. We will not be bidden.'

'For the freedom of the sea, and for nothing else, we would share your rejoicing, Manannan, son of Lir.'

'When the wind is from the south we gallop north. No shores confine us. Be warned. We fly on till the mountains stand across our path and the winds wheel around the world.'

'That is enough for us. We ask nothing that you do not freely give. We demand no shore but where you wish to go. The wind is high and the horses of Manannan are galloping. May we ride with you?'

'Because you are not afraid, you may gallop with us. Because you love the wind, we will carry you. But know this. The seas beneath are deep. To fear is to founder.'

'And to have faith is to race with joy!'

Finnglas was already running into the water, wading out to the wave-tossed manes of the deep.

'You mean, *that's* how we're crossing the sea?' Niall cried in alarm. 'We've got to ride *those* white horses?'

151

'The horses of Manannan wait for no one.'
'*Save me, oh God! For the waters have come up to my neck,*'
sang Niall, and launched himself into the sea after Finnglas.

38

Through channels and coastings and crossings, into the spring silver of the wide North Sea. The wild horses of Manannan galloped on in a surging silence, under the whistling of the wind. Fragments of icebergs, melting in the sun, and the rainbowed sun itself softening above a white sea-mist. All the bitter snow and ice of winter was being gathered up into the blue bosom of the sky. Finnglas and Niall raced high on two sparkling wave-crests. Whales lifted curious heads around them, then flipped the huge flukes of their tails up into the air. Shoals of mackerel darted beneath them, breaking the surface ahead like a scatter of sequins. Gannets dived. Far from the Summer Isle the sea-horses began to slow, running shoulder to shoulder in long, steady lines over deep, crystal-green depths.

A line of blue on the horizon. Sand, heaths and forests waited for them. A quiet land. Few fishing-boats at work, few men in the fields. It was a land that waited for its army to return. Still waiting for its king to come home from the war.

With barely a whisper now, the horses swept Finnglas and Niall up on to the shore, pawed at the sand and cantered seaward again. The wind was wheeling them to the east, to colder coasts and fiords further still.

For a while the two riders lay dumb as driftwood. Then Niall started to sit up.

'We haven't thanked them. Quick, before they're out of earshot.'

Finnglas caught his hand swiftly.

'No! They were going, and we galloped with them. They will not be bidden and they will not be thanked.'

She got to her feet and waved, with her eyes far out to sea.

'Manannan, son of Lir, farewell! Finnglas of the Horses gives you God-speed. May the wind be ever blowing and the tides be running till we meet again.'

Niall raised his hand too and watched the white horses scudding round the headland out of sight. He shook his head, breathing deeply, still trying to hold in his artist's eye the wonder of their sea-skimming gallop.

'So that's how Arthmael lives, when he's not with us!'

'Partly,' said Finnglas. 'Sometimes you see him riding the bow-wave of a ship for the sheer joy of it. Or dancing between the sea and the sky. But there is another world below the surface, that we hardly know of, where he is most at home.'

Saying little, because that ride upon the whales' road had been too wonderful for words to tell of, they walked along the beach. Always afterwards they shared this secret, remembered sometimes on a windy day in the meeting of eyes. Presently Niall said, 'We may need other helpers now. We must ask Arthmael for orders.'

He was just lifting his hand to his mouth to call, when a dark, sleek head popped out of the water in front of him, as though the Dolphin had been waiting for them.

'How long have you been there?' asked Niall suspiciously.

'As long as you have. Or since the sea began. What does it matter as long as I am here when you need me?'

'That's just it,' said Finnglas. 'You can't come with us where we are going now. If the story the geese told Erc is true, then our way lies far inland, to mountains, and an underground cave, to a land-locked lake and a castle. How can you help us there?'

'Oh, Finnglas! How long have you known me?'

'Three years.'

The bright eyes stared back into hers.

'And in all that time, wherever you were, have I ever left you alone?'

'No,' she said in a low, grateful voice.

154

'Nor will I ever. In every age and every element. In every land and none. By many names and many shapes you will know me. Yet I will always be the same.'

'I don't understand. How *can* you follow where we are going?'

His eyes twinkled reproachfully at her. 'You've hurt my feelings, Finnglas. I was rather hoping you were going to follow *me*.'

'But you're a Dolphin!'

Arthmael watched them both hopefully.

Then Niall spoke slowly. 'But . . . that's not *all* you are.'

Arthmael smiled at Niall, as only a dolphin can smile, then danced for joy. He pirouetted on his tail and dived beneath the water.

'Where's he gone?' cried Niall.

'What did he mean?' asked Finnglas.

A head bobbed up on the far side of a rock.

'Arthmael?' called Niall. 'Arth . . . '

But it was only the small, friendly face of a seal that winked back at him.

'I'm sorry,' said Niall. 'I thought . . . '

'That I was Arthmael?' The seal barked with laughter. 'He is not here. He is far ahead of you! You'll have to hurry if you want to keep up with him. Turn around.'

They spun landward. A herd of ponies was trotting down the beach towards them. The Northmen's sturdy little horses, clever-footed, brave. They were not wild, but no one was with them. Finnglas and Niall looked at each other with rising hope.

'Do you suppose they know the way?' asked Finnglas.

'In a land as empty as this there will only be one road north,' Niall answered.

The ponies did not speak, but they crowded round the newcomers, willing and eager-eyed. Finnglas chose the two strongest. They were bay-coloured, with black manes and feet. The riders swung themselves up and their horses trotted up the dunes. The other ponies closed around them, as though to shield the strangers from curious eyes. For a

155

while the herd flowed inland, till the farmland ended in heath and stony scrub.

They reached the road. White-pebbled, open, cutting its way between the trees ahead. The riderless horses wheeled away and cantered back to the fields, to roll on shaggy backs, kicking their hooves in the air as though hope was returning with the newly-springing grass.

More soberly, Finnglas and Niall's mounts trotted north.

'Do you think anyone will stop us?' asked Niall.

'There doesn't seem to *be* anyone. It's as though the land's half dead.'

Just then a streak of white flew past. A wave of warm air went over them, like a hot wind out of the south.

'What was that?'

The white flash sped on, dwindling in the distance till it halted on a distant ridge. It seemed to turn its head to look at them, then vanished over the other side.

Finnglas shivered, remembering the Rhymester's Guard. 'Do you suppose that was a wolf?'

Niall swallowed down his own fear. 'Arthmael sent us by this road and gave us horses. We must take the way it went.'

They topped the rise cautiously. The road dipped and climbed again in front of them, running through woodland dotted with brimming blue lakes. The white figure was still running on ahead.

'Wolf, or Wolfhound?' mused Niall.

It was too distant to be sure, but still they followed.

The road forked, one track running east, back to the distant sea.

'Whatever it is, it's still going north,' said Niall.

Finnglas turned her head. They looked steadily at each other. 'Then we must follow it still.'

'Aye. To the end of the earth, if we have to.'

For half a day that figure ran in front of them, through puddles that reflected the sky. Suddenly, with a single bark, it veered into the birchwoods beside the road. For a moment Niall and Finnglas checked. Then, without a word spoken, they both kicked their ponies to the right and bounded into the tree-cover. For a while they stood in silence, peering through the screening branches. There came the distant clatter of hooves on stone, the tramp of feet, the creaking of wheels.

A slow procession came past them, heavy with gloom. A tattered escort of horsemen, their armour hacked and bloody. Behind them, a gold-helmeted, grey-bearded king, grimly erect, his horse weary under the weight of gilded trappings. Finnglas stiffened. Six months ago she had stood a prisoner in Jarlath's hall and listened with horror as that king had claimed her for his wife.

Spearmen, too few for comfort. Larsa's father, Witgan, limped among them, though the watchers did not know him. Then a heavy cart, shrouded with curtains. Deep in its shadows, hidden from the sunlight, a figure bowed and gaunt almost to exhaustion. But the Rhymester's hands still gripped his skull-decorated staff. With its power he held Jarlath's mind like a shadow of his own, held the king's body stiff upon his horse, held his heart full of hate. He kept the Wolves in their guise even in their reckless pursuit after Pangur. He kept the Worm in its blind malice guarding the caves. Kept the Raven huge and hungry for blood. Held many creatures of doom in hideous shapes and many spells of suffering. Well for the watchers that he did, just then. If his power had not been mightily bent elsewhere he could not have failed to sense the gaze of strangers.

The cart stuck. For swearing, scaring moments, the foot-soldiers struggled to shoulder it free. Then they stumbled on down the long road towards Senargad.

'Is the war over? What does this mean for the prisoners?' whispered Finnglas, testing her sword.

Niall shook his head. When the road was empty again they rode on more warily.

The next ridge showed them the battlefield. Smoke from many pyres stained the sky. Bergenring was coming back to claim its dead. One stack of wood reared higher than all the rest. A black pelt was spread upon the body. The air around it was full of lamentations.

157

'I don't understand,' said Niall. 'Who's won?'

'Jarlath, I suppose. He's driven Bergenring back across his borders. I think their king is dead. But Senargad has suffered heavily too.'

'Where are the wolves?'

Just then a black shadow swept over them, darkening all the land around. The air chilled instantly, as though winter had returned. They looked up and their breath caught in alarm. A gigantic raven was winging over their heads. Blood streaked its beak and talons.

'Mourn! Mourn!' it cawed as it wheeled to the east.

'Where did the Hound go?' asked Finnglas quickly. 'If it *was* a hound.'

Niall scanned the road ahead, the battlefield, and then the mountain slopes.

'There!'

The Hound was leaping up the steep side of the hill towards a high pass. With a surge of relief, Finnglas and Niall urged their horses after it, glad to turn away from the bloody battlefield. For a while there was only the slither of hooves and the laboured breathing of the ponies.

Then, 'Look where he's leading us!' cried Finnglas, hauling in sharply on her horse's mane as she pointed.

Where the pass cut a saddle against the sky the first wolf stood waiting.

39

The Wolfhound threw up its head as it saw the wolves.
Without checking its stride it veered very slightly to the left.
They were galloping now across the high shoulder of the hill.
Finnglas kicked her heels into her mount and glanced up
towards the pass. The hillside was alive with wolves. They
came flowing through the heather and between the boulders
like a grey inundation. Even their powerful strides could not
catch the Hound. But they had seen an easier prey. They
turned diagonally downhill to cut off Finnglas and Niall.

The little horses threw their utmost into flight. Finnglas
crouched low over her pony's neck, till their two straining bodies seemed almost like one. Big Niall, like the
farm-labourer's son he was, bounced and bumped more
uncomfortably. But his pony breathed great chestfuls of the
mountain air and flung both himself and his rider forward
valiantly. The ground was becoming wetter underfoot. Mud
flew from the hooves. The mountainside was running with
myriads of rivers. Snow was collapsing on the peaks.

Over the shoulder of the mountain a wide black mouth
gaped in front of the Hound. The running dog was a white
streak against its shadow.

'The Serpent's cave!' gasped Finnglas. 'The prisoners
are there.'

But as she spoke darkness swooped over them for a
second time. Wings blackened the snow, the sky, the sun.
The great, dire shape of the Rhymester's Raven, huge
feathers outspread, rushed earthwards. It landed before the
tunnel mouth and glared at them with triumph and malice.
Fierce, lightless eyes. Bloodied beak. Curved talons flexed
impatiently as it strutted sideways.

But the Hound laughed as it opened its mouth and sprang faster still between Raven and wolves. Up the next slope and away, on towards the skyline and the dazzle of sunlight.

'Follow it!' panted Niall.

'To eternity!' laughed Finnglas.

The brave ponies wheeled and sped on after it.

Finnglas looked back and saw to her astonishment the wolves, like specks in the heather, still galloping in vain pursuit. The shadow of the Raven lay sharp-edged as a cloak thrown across the landscape, but the two riders were racing clear of it now into open sunshine.

Finnglas eased her mount back to a canter. She said in wonder, 'We've outrun them! We are faster than they are.'

Niall, like his pony, struggled for breath. 'So it's true. They say wolves don't kill by speed but by cunning. They catch the weak and drag them down.'

And then they were over the next crest and a new land lay in front of them.

A lake, like a mirror of polished pewter. A wooden castle close to the shore. A single stone tower. Out of sight of the wolves the horses trotted now, weary but still willing. The white Hound was running eagerly ahead of them down the slope.

They followed it, though with several backward looks.

'But the cave?' questioned Finnglas. 'The prisoners in the cave. Isn't that why we came? To fight the Raven and the wolves, to kill the Worm and rescue our friends?'

'Don't you trust the Hound now?' Niall teased her.

'Of course I do,' Finnglas answered quickly. 'I just don't understand where it's leading us.'

The way dropped into screening forests, with little open patches of pasture and orchards. They began to glimpse bright water through the trees.

A little grey stone farmhouse. From the yard came a sudden commotion of cackling poultry. Then two grey geese ran out across the road. The Hound bent its long head and listened to the urgent gobble of their story. Finnglas and Niall rode up and let their horses stand at rest with drooping heads at last.

'Dwarves! Deceitful cunning creatures!'

'Rude as you like. Slammed the door in our faces.'

'They've not come out since.'

'Not a hide nor a hair of them.'

'There's enchantment there, you mark my words.'

'Well, we had to find somewhere for the winter, didn't we?'

'We've earned our keep, though,' said Brodd proudly. 'Six eggs a week I've laid, and you can't say fairer than that.'

Odd preened his feathers shyly and fell silent. The Hound licked their heads in gratitude and bounded on, down to the lake shore. Finnglas and Niall looked at each other. Without a word they slid from their horses. With a glance at the now-silent farmyard they urged their horses into a nearby meadow and followed the Wolfhound on foot.

It was trotting easily along the stones round the margin, making straight for the point where the castle lay closest to the shore. The drawbridge was raised. There were no sentinels. The land of Bergenring had an empty look, like Senargad.

Between the beach and the island the inlet lay deep and shadowed. Close inshore, the tips of dull green weeds floated on the water. Further out there were darker stirrings, as though something else moved beneath the surface.

The Hound took a flying leap, arching through the air, lean legs stretched out, to land nimbly on the stony platform beside the drawbridge. It wagged its tail and looked hopefully across at them.

'I can't do that!' declared Niall. 'What does it think I am?'

'We can each follow in our own way.'

Finnglas gripped her sword between her teeth. A moment later she had plunged into the water and was swimming strongly.

'No, Finnglas! Not that way! You don't know what's in the lake.'

But Finnglas swam on, out into the brown, murky depths. Niall started to rush into the water after her, then he changed his mind. His hands lifted a huge stone from the beach and held it poised, watching the ripples around Finnglas. Currents darted and twisted on either side of her. Finnglas kept swimming straight and true without looking down. She reached the island and hauled herself up over a boulder to stand beside the drawbridge.

'You see!' she called, with barely a quaver in her voice.

She looked to their guide for approval. But with a last wag of its tail the Wolfhound had vanished. Grimmer now, Finnglas grasped her sword firmly. She turned to stare at the castle behind her and listened. No sound came. With a sudden swinging blow she severed one of the ropes that held the drawbridge. The rustic structure creaked and sagged across the water. Niall stepped back hastily. A second sweep sheared the other rope and the bridge crashed down upon the shore with a sound of splitting timber. Niall gathered up his gown and ran across it before the broken planks had time to decide if they would bear his weight.

They worked swiftly, understanding each other. The great door seemed barred and bolted from within. They moved round the side, close under the shelter of its walls. Ducking below windows that stayed firmly closed, working their way to the farthest point that looked across the lake.

They came, as Sigi and Hygd had done six months before, to the stone tower, and the low door. Once more it opened. Finnglas stooped to explore.

It was as though they had thrust a stick into a wasps' nest. A hundred hands seemed to shoot out of the shadows, pricking them, grasping them, pulling them, dragging them down into the dark. No chance to use a sword or throw a stone. They were tumbled pell-mell down the steps, on into a vast, stone-flagged room. A great kitchen fire blazed. A table was spread with knives, hatchets, hooks, and skewers. A dumpy dwarf-woman, like a hairy boulder, stood in front of the fire holding a hot ladle and grinning at them.

Fifty dwarves surrounded them. Their leaders pinned them to the table. Feet kicked and stamped on them. Hands pinched and pulled and twisted them.

Grinni sprang on to a stool and stood leering down at them.

'Thieves! Cheats! Trespassers! Did you think you would creep into the queen's castle when she wasn't looking? Did you hope you would get your hands on Grinni's treasures? Did you dream you had fooled the dwarves of Bergenring? Oh, wait till Thidrandi hears of this. Wait till the Bear has you between his paws!'

'No! Listen!' Finnglas's voice came almost suffocated beneath the arms of her captors. She fought to make them hear her. 'I am a queen myself now. I have mountains rich with gold. I have no need to rob you. But I bring grimmer news than that. You have been too long in your castle of silence. Don't you know what has happened in the Borderlands?'

The grip of many hard hands seemed to slacken round them. Niall found he could sit up.

'News!'

'What news?'

'Has the battle with Jarlath begun again?'

'Begun and ended. Have you not heard? Do you not know? Your King Thidrandi is dead.'

In the long hall of the castle the dwarves had dragged
out many more carved chests. Hygd moved among them
through the patches of sunlight from the windows. She
would kneel by one, throwing back the heavy lid and
dipping her hands deep into the piled treasure of jewels. She
drew out necklaces, rings, bracelets, coronets. She gave little
gasps and murmurs of pleasure as she lifted each one up to
the light. She held them swaying so that the gold and silver
and precious stones winked at her. Her arms, her neck, her
hair were loaded with jewelry, making her move awkwardly,
stiffly, more like a puppet than a living girl.

Further down the hall Sigi was busy with a similar
game. His toys were weapons, armour, helmets, shields, all
cunningly fashioned by master craftsmen of the rarest metals
and finest gems. He tried the shields on his arm and cut the
dusty air with the swords.

Neither of them once looked at each other, still less out of
the window. They had not seen how the ice was giving way,
letting in the blue sky, how the water was rising. They never
looked to see what might come swimming over its surface.
The only sound was the chink of gold and the swish of blades
and the little greedy gasps.

Suddenly there was a rush of footsteps on the stairs. A
torrent of voices loud with anger. The door burst open.

Both boy and girl reacted with the same movement.
Sweeping a handful of treasures to their bodies. Hiding it,
cradling it, slamming shut the lid of the chest behind them.
They crouched, like two puppies each with a bone, staring
defiantly at the furious crowd of dwarves. Grinni swept them
aside and flung the chests open.

'The time for play is over! These weapons shall see war at last. The dwarves must arm themselves!'

Horny hands were delving in from every side.

In the midst of a seething sea of hairy dwarves two figures stood out above the rest. A tall girl in a tunic and breeches, with brown hair tied back from a sea-tanned face and hazel eyes eager for adventure. An ox of a young man in a white monk's gown, with half-shaved head and huge, clever hands.

The girl cried out and came across the hall with running strides.

'Can it be Hygd? And are you Sigi? Have we truly found the first of those we seek?'

But Hygd backed away, clutching all the jewels she could. The dwarves were pulling out breastplates, chain mail, helmets, weapons of every sort.

'No! No!' gasped Sigi, darting to and fro as he tried to stop them putting on their own handiwork.

Niall watched the children, and his smile of joy grew suddenly grim.

'Pray Odin we're in time,' growled Grinni. 'It'll be wet work in the tunnels by the look of it.'

He held out weapons and armour to Niall and Finnglas. His eyes sparkled with a strange excitement.

'Go on!' he urged. 'You will not see workmanship like these in the Summer Isle. No sword can cut these coats, no spear strike through them, not even spells can pierce the heart of those who wear them.'

Two coats of mail dangled before their eyes. One slender, moon-silver for Finnglas, one bronze, immensely broad for Niall's huge back. Finnglas, armed only with her new queen's sword, reached out with eyes alight. She stroked the supple, swaying links and felt its lightness in her hand.

'You are right! Rare is the craft that fashioned this. I have never seen strength like it, and I do not doubt its powers.'

Already she was lifting it, ready to slip it over her head.

In his other hand, Grinni waved the bronze corselet at Niall. But the young monk stepped back. His hand grasped the wooden cross on his wide chest. He shook his head in a movement that was half a laugh and half a shudder.

'No, thank you!'

The dwarf's eyes grew dark and very bright.

'Take it, I say!'

'I'll trust my life to no dwarves' magic. What would a monk do in a suit of armour? A fine fool I'd look.'

Forgetting Finnglas now, the dwarf took a step nearer. The other dwarves were crowding round. They looked as though at any moment they might rush the big monk and force the armour over his head. Niall's eyes swung round the group with a flash of sudden understanding.

'So that's the way of it? You thought you'd trick us like these children before us, did you? Well, there is one Fool I'll gladly take the side of. This is all the armour I need!'

With one big hand he held his cross up in front of their eyes. With the other he dashed the coat of mail from Grinni's grip. As it clashed on the floor the dwarves let out a howl of rage. For a bewildered moment Finnglas stared at him. Then, not without a wince of regret, she threw her shining silver chain mail after it.

'A coat of magic mail indeed! Traitors! No spells to threaten us from outside, but a mighty one to bind us yours from within. My thanks, Niall! You were wiser than I was. What shall we do with them now?'

She drew her sword threateningly. The dwarves cursed and chattered.

'It was a great gift.'

'You'll be sorry when you see what dangers wait in the tunnels.'

'What can your cross do against the Serpent, eh?'

But Niall was not listening. In three big strides he was across the room and grasping Sigi by the arm. The boy's protests were no more than the squeaking of a bat as Niall tore off the imprisoning coat of mail, struck the sword from his hand, tossed the shield till it spun against the wall. Finnglas was doing the same with Hygd, stripping the shrieking little girl of all her borrowed jewels.

166

The dwarves watched in a grim, glum silence. The children yelled and hiccuped and fell silent. Then Sigi yawned and rubbed his eyes and opened them very wide.

'Who are you?' he asked, as if seeing them for the first time.

'Queen Finnglas, and this is my soul-friend Niall. We have come to save your sister Larsa. But it seems she is not the only one in danger.'

Hygd was staring about her with a puzzled frown.

'Where are we? Who are all these funny little men? And what's the matter with Larsa?'

Niall picked her up in his strong arms.

'It's a long, dark story, little Hygd. But it shall have a happy ending if Finnglas and I have anything to do with it.'

Finnglas held her sword pointed firmly at Grinni's chest.

'Well? Our mission is urgent, and so is yours. We will not enter the Borderlands as your prisoners. But shall we call a truce, and march together as allies in good faith? You to rescue your prince, and we our friends?'

The armed dwarves exchanged ominous glances. Niall pushed Sigi and Hygd back behind him. Then Grinni scowled and turned for the door.

'There are scores to be settled. Don't think we'll forget this. But if we're not quick there'll be nothing but drowned corpses to find in those tunnels.'

He set off at a trot, down the winding stairs. Finnglas turned to the children.

'Wait here for us. We'll be back with Larsa and Mai as swiftly as we can.'

Hygd clung to her. 'No! Don't leave us alone! I'm frightened now.'

Over their heads Finnglas's eyes met Niall's. He shrugged.

'As safe with us as anywhere in times like these . . . But stay close behind me, and do exactly what I say,' he ordered Sigi and Hygd.

They ran down the steps behind the dwarves. At the door of her kitchen the hairy Grid in her apron watched them go by. She waved her ladle over her head like a banner.

41

They went down and down, past the foot of the tower stairs and deeper still. For lamps the dwarves had moonstones and pearls in their helmets that glowed from within with a pale, unearthly light. They turned into a low, straight tunnel, floored with slime. The walls dripped water. Grinni looked at the leading dwarves with a grimace between a smile and a scowl.

'There is a lakeful of water over our heads and filling fast. Even the dwarf-roads may not hold out this time.'

'Stop yattering and get a move on, unless you want to be caught under here when the roof gives.'

'Once we reach the middle, there can be no turning back.'

'And no saying what will happen under the mountain if the river breaks through.'

'Can we trust the old road, the high road, the dry road?'

'We have to find it first. And I trust nothing and nobody.'

'For King and cunning!'

'New king. Old cunning, eh?'

All the time their feet were slopping forward in the slime.

Towards the back of the line Finnglas twisted her head upwards. She did not like to be last and it was uncomfortable to be hurrying forward while having to stoop so low. It was worse for Niall. His broad shoulders rubbed the greasy walls. Did the stones creak above their heads? Were the cracks wider? Did the water trickle faster down their necks?

Sigi and Hygd were quiet now, half-running behind them with quick breaths that might have been either sobs or pantings. Presently Sigi gave a little cry and looked back.

'I think something's following us.'

In one swift movement Finnglas scooped the children forward in front of Niall's protective bulk and stood facing the rear with her drawn sword in her hand. Above the growl of the dwarves' voices up ahead and the sucking of their feet in the slime another sound came echoing along the curving walls.

Slap. Squelch. Slap. Squelch.

Far from the light of the dwarves' helmets a faint pallor in the gloom was coming round the bend. For an aching moment Finnglas hoped it might be the white Hound and strove to calm her fears. But it was not. This was something greyer. No, two shapes. Marching steadily, bearing down on her. Finnglas raised her sword. The shapes gobbled as they came.

'I told you. There they are!'

'If they're not quick, we'll all be swimming for it.'

'I'm a gander, not a water-rat. Give me fresh air and green grass, any day.'

'It's Odd and Brodd!' cried Hygd, breaking free from Niall and running back to throw her arms round the goose's neck.

'Where have you been, you dears? It's been so long since we saw you.'

'Hmph! And who's fault is that? Not so much as a crust tossed out of the window. We might have starved or frozen for all you noticed.'

'Oh, Brodd! You're *fat*.'

'No thanks to you two. I've worked for my corn.'

'What's that?'

'Who's there?'

Dwarves were turning aggressively, weapons winking in the stone-light.

'Friends. Valiant allies,' called Finnglas.

'It's Odd and Brodd. They saved our lives from the wolves,' reported Hygd.

'But what are you doing here?' asked Sigi.

'We heard you were going to find Mai, our goose-girl. Right! Then we're coming too,' said Odd proudly.

169

'Faster,' ordered Grinni.

Water was trickling along the tunnel floor now. Black coils weaving and writhing through the slime. Then creeping above it. Beginning to merge and fatten like dark, slithering snakes, twining coldly round their ankles.

'No talking. Save your breath for running.'

The whole column of dwarves broke into a trot. Weapons and armour clanked. Feet splashed. And the noise of the rising river was growing stronger all the time.

Niall's hands grasped Sigi and Hygd on either side and hurried them along.

'I'm sorry, Hygd,' he panted. 'I'd carry you on my shoulders if I could, but the roof is too low.'

It was hardest for him. The tunnel was cut for dwarves not a third his size. He had to run with his head stuck out in front of him like a charging bull.

'What will we do if the water fills this tunnel?' gasped Sigi.

'Die as we would wish to live,' answered Finnglas. 'Bravely.'

'We must be almost out from under the lake,' Niall tried to cheer them. 'The tunnel's rising.'

But the water came flowing faster than ever. They were scrambling almost on all fours now. There seemed to be steps ahead, but the flood was swirling down them like a waterfall. They floundered up them and halted suddenly.

There was a press of dwarves filling the tunnel, unmoving. Voices were beginning to rise in panic. Over their heads Finnglas and Niall caught the gleam of cold, colourless light on a scene of devastation. The roof of the chamber rose, held up on old wooden pit props, shiny with slime. More logs had been lashed to them, making a lattice of scaffolding and platforms that stretched up into darkness. It should have been easier walking now, with the low, suffocating tunnel past. But a barrier blocked the way. A great tidal wave of glistening shingle had been swept across the cavern, piled up against the scaffolding like a black snowdrift. And all the time the chilly water was forcing its way between the stones,

170

washing them forward with the relentless force of a moving glacier. Already they could feel the sting of gravel against their legs, the weight of stones and water dragging at their knees. It was up to the dwarves' waists.

Grinni swung round on his nearest companions.

'We may have come too late to find them alive. We'll be lucky to get out of this with our own lives.'

'Dare we try the Old Gallery?'

A shiver of fear ran through them all.

'There is only one way out bar this, and we all know where *that* leads.'

'The Serpent of Senargad will never let the dwarves of Bergenring past alive.'

The wall of debris groaned and moved forward, pressing against the ancient scaffolding.

'We have no choice. We cannot go back now. In a few moments that tunnel will be filled for ever.'

Grinni swung himself on to the scaffolding and started to climb. A moment later, Niall was seizing the dripping dwarves round the waist and hoisting them on to the ladders. Tall Finnglas waited till the last, while the props creaked and shifted and the sounds of scrambling went higher and higher over her head. Sigi and Hygd hung just above them, not wanting to leave them far behind. At last, Finnglas and Niall began to climb after the dwindling pinpoints of the lamps. Finally Odd and Brodd came flapping heavily up from perch to perch, like roosting poultry.

High in the shadows of the roof a crack opened through which they squeezed themselves. Niall gave a great shout that rang above the excited cries of the dwarves. The light that had fallen cool and pale as moonbeams now sprang back in a brilliant multitude of colours. On all sides of them sparkled seams of quartz and precious jewels.

Every dwarf's hand flew to the pick he carried in his belt. Their eyes shone bright as the crystal stones themselves. But Grinni sprang to face them.

'No! Would you fall thrall to the dwarves' own spell? These jewels will still be here in a million years. But I fear

171

that it may be too late already to find those we came to seek still alive. Run!'

And he darted off along the dazzling gallery.

'What did he mean?' panted Sigi. 'Is he talking about Mai and Larsa? Are they dead?'

'Be brave,' said Finnglas, grasping his hand. 'As they were.'

But her own heart was aching for Erc and Pangur Bán.

The glitter of gems streaked ahead of them like shafts of lightning. The gallery was dry and the floor was sound and sure at last. They ran, to a steady pounding of feet and the rasp of panting, with the geese flapping behind.

Suddenly Grinni flung up his hand and the column halted. The dwarf's face was frowning and he cupped his hand to a large ear. They struggled to still their laboured breathing and strained to listen. Between their hammering heartbeats they heard it at last. The muffled, far-off sound of singing.

42

'Though strong walls surround,
And monsters appal us,
Our hearts are unbound;
No fears shall enthral us.'

The flood-surge was crowding the raft ever closer under the roof. Their fingers were torn and bleeding with clinging on to the rock lest they be sucked down and under past the last pocket of air. But still they shouted defiantly into the swirling darkness. Pangur's high voice rose above the rest. Larsa and Mai joined in lustily, with Oslaf stamping out the rhythm and threatening to swamp the boat until they made him stop. At first Kara had clamped her lips in furious contempt, but now even she gasped out the lines of hope and courage. What else could they do?

'Though cruelty cover us,
Yet speak not of dying.
While deep waves roll over us
Our faith is still flying.'

A loud crack echoed in their ears. The brave song broke off and they looked up in sudden alarm.

'The roof!' squeaked Pangur. 'Is it giving way?'

Despair struggled in their faces. Was their last dwindling refuge about to collapse about them? From directly over Oslaf's head came the sound of violent hammering. A chip of rock bounced on to the prince's forehead, drawing a trickle of blood. They crouched lower in the boat, wet and shivering, shielding their heads with raised arms. Over them

173

now a crack was widening. They watched the deepening fissure, waiting every moment for the last rush of water from above that would drown them. The hammering became more urgent.

'Listen!' hissed Pangur. 'It's not water.'

There was the ring of metal on stone, many-tongued, like a chime of ill-tuned bells.

'Is someone there?' Kara breathed the words.

They looked at each other with a joy beyond hope.

In the hush below the distant roar of voices came through the crack, like the rumble of surf.

Then, 'Help!' bellowed Oslaf.

And 'Help!' cried Larsa and Mai.

The many hammer-blows broke off, the voices stilled. Then bedlam broke out. Fragments of rock came crashing down around them, but the survivors hardly noticed as they shouted with relief. Larsa sheltered Pangur on her lap as best she could. The tip of a pick broke through, and then half a dozen more. Light flowed down, brilliant, into the gold-sparkling darkness. Hands reached, groped, grasped for them.

'Hold on to my ankles!'

'Lower away.'

'Hold him tight while he takes the strain.'

Into the glittering cavern rose Mai's white, pock-marked face. The geese squawked with joy.

Then Larsa followed, clutching Pangur in her strong arms.

'Finnglas!'

With a mew of gratitude Pangur flung himself into the young queen's arms.

'And Niall too! What are you doing here? I thought I left you in the Summer Isle. But, oh, I've never been so glad to see you!'

'Does no one remember that I am a princess?' complained a voice from below.

Then Kara too was whisked up through the sharp-sided shaft.

Down in the gloom the flood tugged at the raft. Lightened of its load, the skin-boat was almost swept away before Oslaf too was hauled to safety. He stood in the light, grinning shyly at everyone.

There was much hugging of friends. Larsa embraced Hygd and Sigi. Odd and Brodd were cackling for happiness as they flapped round Mai. But fifty dwarves threw themselves prostrate on the floor before Oslaf.

'What is this?' snapped Kara. 'A princess expects greetings but not grovellings.'

No one took any notice of her. Grinni lifted his head and looked full in the young man's bewildered face.

'Hail, Oslaf of Bergenring! The honour falls to the dwarves to be the first to salute you as our king.'

Oslaf's mouth fell open in a worried grin.

'Oh, no. You've got it wrong. I'm only a prince.'

'*Only* a prince!' hissed Kara. 'Is that not dignity high enough?'

The dwarf-captain raised himself upon one knee, and shook his head grimly.

'Prince no longer. I bring you heavy news, your Majesty. Your father marched to war against King Jarlath and found a noble death upon the battlefield. The crown of Bergenring is yours. The Bear is dead. Long live the Bear-cub!'

Oslaf brushed a tear from his eye.

'My father! Me? King! Oh, I can't. No, really, I couldn't. I wasn't even good enough at being a prince.'

'Nonsense!' A hand gripped his own firmly. A tall figure stood proudly beside him, head uplifted. 'Have you not done all that a prince should do these last six months? You fought the Serpent. You brought back the skin that saved us all. You have led us to safety here without thought of fear. Do not doubt now, your Majesty. As king, you shall do greater things still, with Kara of Senargad beside you as your queen.'

It was a long speech for Oslaf's puzzled brain to understand. But he saw Kara, pale but smiling, felt her lift his hand to her lips and bestow a kiss upon it. The truth dawned on his face in a dazzling smile.

'You mean, you'll marry me!'

'Do you imagine you could manage without me?' Then Kara went down on one knee demurely. 'Kara of Senargad accepts the honour of Bergenring's hand.'

'You see?' whispered Mai triumphantly. 'I told you people could change.'

Greatly daring, Oslaf lifted her to her feet and kissed her face.

Two spots of colour flared on Kara's cheeks. But she turned abruptly to the dwarves.

'We thank you for this gallant rescue. News must be taken to my father instantly, and peace made between our lands. Can you take us to safety?'

The dwarves' faces grew dark and they muttered to each other. Grinni spoke for all of them.

'It's a pity you didn't give him your hand sooner, your Highness. The floods have blocked the way to Bergenring for ever. The only way now lies forward to Senargad.'

'And the Rhymester's Worm is guarding that.'

The dwarves drew their swords and settled their shields upon their arms. They formed themselves on either side of Oslaf and Kara.

'Lead forward, your Majesty. The dwarves of Bergenring will die beside you.'

43

Slipping and scraping themselves painfully, Erc and Bor scrambled up the wall after the Worm. The golden slime clung to their hands and hair, and the reek of the thick, black blood was on everything.

Suddenly there was nothing above them. The Worm had gone. Even the sound of his painful passage was stilled. The roar and rush of the rising flood filled the cavern, battering their senses. Erc and Bor were too out of breath to speak to each other, but they climbed on, wary now of what lay in wait for them over their heads.

The vertical glitter of gold ended. There was a wide opening, where roof and wall did not quite meet. Beyond must be a level, unseen surface. The Worm-light pricked the darkness above it only faintly, like a lamp in a mist.

Erc levered himself up on his elbows. He heard Bor breathing heavily beside him. They crawled over the edge and crouched cautiously.

The Worm had halted. They could make out his dark bulk where the trail ended. They could hear the hiss and suck of his breath. Dimly they saw the blind head turning, scenting. The dreadful words rasped out.

'I s-s-see you.'

The shadows could not hide them from him, who did not need the light.

'You s-s-struck me. You s-s-skinned me! You s-s-stole it from me.'

He was twisting now, lashing his wounded tail with gasps of self-inflicted pain. The long neck swung his head from side to side. Claws raked the rock. They could not back away. There was only the drop into the flood behind them. The

177

cavern was wide, but the Worm's scaly coils filled it. They tried to creep towards the wall. But though his eyes could not discern them, he sensed where they were.

'You s-s-shall not es-s-scape. I s-s-shall have revenge.'

'It wasn't us that hurt you.'

Bor startled them all with the sound of his own voice.

'Humans-s-s! They are all the s-s-same. What does-s-s it matter which of you pays-s-s for my hurts-s-s?'

The shadow was lurching nearer, covering the gold light. Erc's muscles stiffened. Should they make a dash for it, in a wild hope to squeeze past that monstrous bulk, round it, under it even, in a bid for freedom? Or dive back where they had come into the chilling waters?

He sensed a great clawed foot raised.

'Help!' yelled Bor. 'Save us!'

A white shape came skimming through the cave like the passing of a moth's wings. The Serpent reared. Suddenly, beneath its belly, they saw daylight in front of them. A glimpse of melting snow, reviving grass, a clear blue sky.

Then, 'Gore! Gore!' came a hideous cry.

Blackness descended again across the tunnel mouth. There was a battering of heavy wings that thrummed the air and drove the Serpent's stench towards them. The shuffling of taloned feet outside the cave.

'The Raven of Death,' groaned Bor. 'That's it. We're finished now.'

But the white Hound and the glimpse of day had given Erc hope. He grasped Bor's unwilling hand and edged nearer the Worm.

'Don't be so sure!' he said, lifting his head to listen.

The Worm had heard it too. He held the cruel foot suspended and groped his head towards the darkest end of the cavern. There was a faint echo of voices and the tramp of many feet.

'What's happened to the light? We seem to have left that wall of jewels behind,' came a ringing call.

'Niall?' breathed Erc in wonder.

A sharp cry, and then Kara's pained complaint.

'A princess does not expect to pick her way through mine-shafts.'

Another girl's voice came brisk and cheerful.

'Speak for yourself. A princess may do as she pleases. But a true queen must walk harder roads than this for the sake of her people.'

'And Finnglas too!' marvelled Erc.

'We should be getting near daylight by now. What's happened to the tunnel entrance?' said a deep, gruff voice.

'There!'

'Look!'

'Is that the Serpent? Help!'

An unmistakable, unlooked-for mew that could only be Pangur.

They marched into the cave. There was a great crowd of them. So many familiar faces that Erc had never hoped to see again.

Niall's huge height was evident at once, and Finnglas too, with the light of battle in her face. And, oh joy, there in the centre was Larsa, pale but unhurt, with Sigi and Hygd on either side of her. Close by, a pock-marked girl in rags, flanked by two geese. And surely that was the Princess Kara herself. At the head of them all, his moon-face lit by the upturned helmets of two ranks of dwarves, walked Oslaf.

Two cries rang out from the boys to greet them. *'Help us!'*

'Bor!' cried Sigi and Hygd.

'It's Erc!' shrilled Pangur.

But between those two and the rest sprawled the coils of the vindictive Serpent. And barring the mouth of the cave was the Raven of Death. Finnglas stepped forward and raised her sword.

In the darkened room of a tower in Senargad, the Rhymester stiffened. He reached a black-nailed hand from the fold of his sleeve and drew towards him the head of a giant toad. He parted the shrivelled skin. Deep in its cleft skull glowed a dark-red jewel. The Rhymester's fingers gripped the edge of the table as he bent and stared at the scene that was forming in it.

179

In a pale silver light the ranks of Bergenring advanced towards the gold and black Worm of Senargad. The shadowy figures of Erc and Bor flattened themselves against the wall close behind it. There was perilously little room between the Serpent's stirring tail and the edge of the drop.

The dwarves came on, led by Finnglas and Oslaf and Grinni, with drawn swords.

'I s-s-see you,' screamed the Serpent, twisting this way and that.

'War! War!' shrieked the Raven, hungry for blood.

'Now!' yelled Grinni, and rushed forward, leading the charge.

A great foot slammed down, crushing a dwarf to the ground. But swords had pierced the Worm's skin and he bellowed in pain.

The Rhymester smiled in satisfaction.

Again the dwarves hurled themselves into the fray. Oslaf struck out bravely. This time the Serpent lashed from wall to wall and sent six more of them spinning senseless. The attackers drew back muttering. But the Worm was wounded too. Finnglas looked down. The floor beneath her feet was slippery with blood.

The Rhymester's breath hissed as he watched her face in the depths of the jewel. He began to plait a noose of sinews and hair, tugging the knot ever tighter.

Finnglas gripped her sword. Once more, grim-faced, they drove against him. One claw ripped into Finnglas's shoulder, tearing her cloak away. The Worm was stabbed in many places now. He lifted his blind head and howled vainly.

'I s-s-see you. I s-s-see you all.'

The Rhymester lit a heap of choking herbs. The smoke went creeping out under the doorway.

'Well?' urged Kara. 'What are you waiting for? Finish him now.'

The air was full of sobbing hisses. The Worm was striking out sightlessly even before they came within reach.

The Rhymester's clawed hands were twisting in suspense. 'Hate!' he urged. 'Hate!'

180

Less willingly now, summoning up their battered courage, the dwarves settled their shields before them. They started a slow, measured advance. In spite of her wound, Finnglas was still at their head.

It was there again. That white flicker through the gloom. That running shape that bounded past them all. It reached the tortured Worm and there the Hound paused. As once before, it bent and licked the bleeding wounds. Then it lifted its head, and they heard its voice. A ghostly howl sorrowed through the shadows.

The Rhymester started from his chair with a screech of rage.

The Hound was gone. Everyone looked at their neighbour doubtfully. The Worm was raising himself on his hind legs, lashing this way and that. The dwarves closed in, long shadows thrown behind them by their lamps. Bor flung himself selflessly on the Worm's threshing tail. Finnglas's sword stabbed out. Suddenly Mai gave an anguished cry.

'No! Stop! Don't hurt him! Didn't you see the Hound?'

She flung herself through the dwarves, sending Finnglas's weapon clattering to the floor. She ran under the tearing claws and threw her arms around the blind Worm's neck. She clung to him and turned to face the others, her eyes running with tears.

'Don't you see? It's wrong! He's as much the Rhymester's prisoner as we are. In all the time we were here, what did he ever do to injure us?'

And she laid her cheek against his face and held him close.

At her touch, the Worm opened his jaws in a harrowing roar.

Finnglas snatched up her sword and sprang forward to save her, with the dwarves ringing round. But there was no way they could strike without injuring Mai. Odd charged, but stopped short with a cackle of grief.

Still the fanged lips gaped wider. Before their horrified gaze the scaly skin began to split. A fissure ran down the rippling body. The Serpent rocked and writhed. The skin was falling away in a dry sheet of scales. And from

181

underneath a new body was emerging. The dull, dark coat was giving way to glistening green and gold, bright as a butterfly newly-hatched, save for his raw, scarred tail. He swung his sightless head and raised a foot, stiffly, to claw away the mask from his face, from his mouth, from his neck.

Mai hugged him closer and kissed the blank, sealed eyes.

Scales cracked apart. The heavy, black lids opened for the first time.

'I can *s-s-see* you!' the Serpent gasped as he gazed at Mai.

She was looking into the most beautiful eyes she had ever seen. A brilliant emerald green, patterned with stars of gold. As clear and vivid as dew-hung grass on the first morning in May in the dawn of the world.

'But you're lovely!' breathed Mai, stroking his shining skin. 'Lovely *and* lovable!'

The Worm looked long at the pock-marked, ragged goose-girl, as though he could never see enough of her.

'And so are you! The loveliest person in the whole world.'

Far away in the palace in Senargad the Rhymester's hood fell forward. One hand clutched his robe over the place where his heart should have been.

'What's happening?' shouted Erc. 'The light! What's happened to the Raven?'

Sunshine was flooding into the cave, dazzling on the gold of the Serpent's coils, dancing on the weapons and armour of the dwarves, catching the cross on the white of Niall's chest and the green of Pangur's eyes, flashing in the smiles of Larsa and Sigi and Hygd.

Something black and glossy strutted to and fro outside the entrance.

'Caw! Caw!' it croaked as it stabbed the sunlit grass.

Just a common raven. A smallish, ordinary bird of prey, hardly bigger than a crow.

The Rhymester's grey robe began to sag. The sleeve hung empty. The skin closed over the toad's dark jewel and it slowly crumbled to dust.

High on the steep mountainside other things were changing. Wolves bounded from boulders and landed awkwardly, surprised. Hairy skins fell away, becoming no more than wolf-cloaks hanging from human shoulders. Claws changed into hands reaching for unfamiliar weapons. Muzzles melted into the metal of helmets.

The eyes of Jarlath's Wolf-Guard looked at each other with alarm, not trusting their memories.

'Where are we?'

'What are we doing here?'

'Where's the . . . *Rhymester* . . . ?'

But the last word seemed to float away and lose itself upon a dying breeze.

In a shuttered room, in the heart of the palace, the smoke eddied and cleared. A grey cloak fell forward on the floor. The folds emptied themselves of air, flattened, settled. For a while two red points burned within the shadow of the hood, growing fainter and fainter, like a fire that is going cold. At last the room was very silent and empty, with the stillness that is peace. A mouse came out of a hole and began to wash its whiskers. Outside the window a robin began to sing.

In the palace courtyard a gloomy Jarlath paused beside the weapon-stone. Suddenly he flexed his shoulders, as if a great burden had fallen from them. He rubbed his eyes and looked around. He seemed to see for the first time the light blue sky with little puffs of white clouds skimming the hilltops, the froth of apple blossom in the orchards, the waters laughing in the sound. The nervous courtiers saw him raise his fist and strike Thor's hammer a mighty blow. A great ringing laugh burst from his grey beard, like the gladness of a man released at last from prison.

'Kara! Where is she hiding? Bring her to me. I want my daughter Kara!'

44

Never had the palace of Senargad seen rejoicing like it. The mead-cup went round from hand to hand. The pipes shrilled and the fiddles skipped. Niall in white and Finnglas in a borrowed gown of crimson and gold vied with each other in a nimble sword-dance, while the dwarves clashed their goblets on the tables and drowned the drums with the hammering of their heels. Bonfires blazed on the hillsides and across the sound Odd and Brodd crooned as they settled to rest in Bilberry's stable.

At the height of the feasting, Kara took Oslaf by the hand.

'Well, your Majesty?' she smiled. 'Will you leap with me into fame and fortune?'

Oslaf gulped, and took a deep breath. 'Oh, yes! Will you?'

'You silly boy! You would never be able to rule your kingdom without me!'

And with a great shout of joy he seized her hand and dragged her forward. Together they leaped high over the flames of the wedding-fire, landing before Jarlath to kiss each other as man and wife.

Oslaf's mother, Queen Suld, wiped a tear from her eye. But King Jarlath embraced them both with a great roar of laughter. The fire threw his shadow behind him. It lay on the floor, the wall, flat, empty, obedient, moving only when he moved. No red eyes burned within its darkness. It did not rule him. King Jarlath was his own man, in his own home.

The Worm lay beside the fire. His magnificent coils of green and gold sparkled in the light as they folded lovingly about Mai.

The soldiers downed their share of beer and wrapped their wolf-cloaks round them carelessly. Unafraid, unfrightening.

Though ever afterwards there was still a little of the wolf in them, as there is in all of us.

Pangur looked up from Sigi's knees and saw Finnglas tap Erc on the shoulder.

'Erc! I've got something important to ask you.'

Erc swung round.

'Oh, Finnglas! There's something wonderful I have to tell you!'

The two of them walked out into the moonlight. The little white cat jumped down and followed them curiously into the cool night air.

Finnglas, being a queen, spoke first.

'Erc. I know the world sees a great difference between us. I a queen, and you a fisherman. But noble deeds make noble men. Last year you rescued Niall and Pangur and me, and now you have risked your life to come back to Senargad for your friends. The Summer Isle too has need of courage like yours to guide and guard it. Erc, I am offering you my hand in marriage and half my throne.'

Pangur heard the surprised gasp from the young fisherman.

'Finnglas! What can I say? You offer me too great an honour . . . And . . . '

'It is an honour richly deserved.'

There were quick steps behind him that halted in the doorway. Erc turned and held out his hand to someone.

'And besides . . . I wanted to tell you. Larsa has agreed to marry me!'

He stepped back into the lamplight. The pot-girl stood beside him, a smile of joy on her broad, strong face, and took his arm.

Pangur winced. There was a startled silence. Then Finnglas broke into laughter and hugged them both. Lifting the gold torque from her throat, she clasped it round Larsa's neck.

'My blessing on the pair of you!'

Grasping them both by the hand, she ran with them into the hall and cried in a ringing voice, 'Glad news, my friends! Tonight, before you all, Larsa and Erc will jump this wedding-fire too and make our circle of joy complete.'

And hand in hand, the fisherman's son and the potter's daughter leaped over the flames into a new life, while everyone shouted with merriment.

When the cheering and stamping had finished the dancing broke out more wildly than ever, with the two new couples leading the reel down the hall. Mai danced with Bor. And then Sigi linked hands with Queen Suld, and Jarlath swung little Hygd right off her feet. But at the height of the dancing Kara slipped away and laid her wedding flowers at the foot of her bed, where faithful Elli had slept. There Oslaf found her, and led her back again to join the feasting.

Someone else was missing too. At midnight Finnglas left the party and walked on the beach to cool her flushed cheeks. Niall and Pangur Bán got up and followed her. They stood at the shoreline, looking out over the moonlit sea. A broad, sleek head lifted under the moon and whistled to them.

Finnglas gasped.

'Arthmael!'

'Is it really you?' cried Niall.

'Who else?'

'But you . . . '

'We didn't know . . . '

'We thought perhaps we would never see you again,' mewed Pangur.

'Really? You were going to consign me to the history books, were you? Did you think you could get rid of the Dancing Fool as easily as that!'

Finnglas knelt down and put her arms around his long, wet head.

'Oh, Arthmael! I'm sorry. I do try to follow you, but I can't always manage it. I was wrong, wasn't I, when I tried to kill the Worm?'

He bent his head and kissed her small, cold nose.

'You loved your friends, Finnglas. You would fight to the death for them. But the way of love may be harder even than that. In the end it was the courage of all of you that gave sight

186

to the Worm, and Kara to Oslaf and Larsa to Erc. The world has need of fools like you.'

He twirled a strand of seaweed round her head with his tail and teased her.

'Are you really in love with Erc?'

Finnglas blushed. 'He saved my life and my honour. I wanted to reward him.'

'Oh, Finnglas!'

'I know. I was an idiot, wasn't I? Larsa will make him much happier than I could ever have.'

She hugged the Dolphin closer.

'Stay with me now, Arthmael. I need you more than ever. It is going to be hard to be a queen alone.'

He swung her right off her feet and tossed her onto his back in the water.

'When did I ever leave you? I have been with you from the beginning, and I always will be.'

'All right! I believe you!' spluttered Finnglas. 'I know that now. Under the sea, or on the highest mountain, or in the deepest darkness beneath the earth. And wherever I find you, in whatever shape you come to me, I will try to dance with you always, I promise.'

'Good! Then what are we waiting for?'

Light spilled from the palace. The pipes were skirling another wedding-reel. Kara and Oslaf, Erc and Larsa, led the laughing lines of dancers. But the Queen of the Summer Isle was long in coming. In the shallow sea, in the brilliant moonlight, Finnglas and Arthmael were dancing now together.

The Worm came slithering over the shingle to join them, with Mai's arm around his neck as she walked beside him. At the water's edge, Niall turned and laughed a greeting. And Pangur Bán rubbed round their legs, miaowing for joy.

Also from Lion Publishing

SHAPE-SHIFTER
The Naming of Pangur Bán

Fay Sampson

Deep in a dark cave in the Black Mountain, a
witch was plotting mischief: 'We need something
small, something sly, to carry a spell . . . and then
we shall see who reigns on the Black Mountain!'

Shape-Shifter, the kitten, is her victim. But,
before the charm is complete, he escapes. He finds
himself caught in a spell that has gone wrong and a
body that is not his own.

In blind panic, he brings disaster even to those
who want to help him. Only a greater power can
break the spell . . .

ISBN 0 7459 1347 4

PANGUR BÁN, THE WHITE CAT

Fay Sampson

The princess Finnglas is in the deadly grip of
the evil Sea Monster, deep down in the mysterious
underwater kingdom of the Sea Witch. And Niall
has been bewitched by the mermaids.

Pangur Bán, the white cat, is desperate. He
must rescue them – but how can he free them from
enchantment?

Only Arthmael can do it. But who is Arthmael?
Where is he? Can Pangur find him in time?

Shortlisted for the *Guardian* Children's Fiction
Award in 1984, this is the second book about
Finnglas and her friends.

ISBN 0 85648 580 2

FINNGLAS OF THE HORSES

Fay Sampson

Dangers, surprises and unexpected happiness lie
ahead for the princess Finnglas as she sets out to
find her beloved horse, Melisant.

For her companions, Niall and Pangur Bán, the
white cat, this desperate quest is an adventure they
will never forget.

This is the third book about Finnglas and her
friends.

ISBN 0 85648 899 2

FINNGLAS AND THE STONES OF CHOOSING

Fay Sampson

'On, Cloud-clearer, on!' screamed the princess
Finnglas. But she knew her horse was already
pouring out all his strength. And the black stallion
was still ahead . . .

Finnglas is riding for her life. If she fails the first
of the Seven Trials to win the kingdom she will
die. And the Summer Land will never be free from
the grip of the Druids and their Powers.

This is the fourth book about Finnglas and her
friends.

ISBN 0 7459 1124 2

A selection of top titles from LION PUBLISHING

KILLER DOG	Peggy Burns	£1.50 ☐
NOTHING EVER STAYS THE SAME	Peggy Burns	£1.75 ☐
SHADOWS IN THE VALLEY	Audrey Constant	£1.95 ☐
NICK AND CO. IN A FIX	Bob Croson	£1.50 ☐
NICK AND CO. ON HOLIDAY	Bob Croson	£1.95 ☐
MEET THE AUSTINS	Madeleine L'Engle	£1.95 ☐
THE MOON BY NIGHT	Madeleine L'Engle	£2.25 ☐
A RING OF ENDLESS LIGHT	Madeleine L'Engle	£2.50 ☐
SHAPE-SHIFTER: THE NAMING OF PANGUR BÁN	Fay Sampson	£1.95 ☐
PANGUR BÁN, THE WHITE CAT	Fay Sampson	£1.50 ☐
FINNGLAS OF THE HORSES	Fay Sampson	£1.50 ☐
FINNGLAS AND THE STONES OF CHOOSING	Fay Sampson	£1.50 ☐
GREYBACK	Eleanor Watkins	£1.95 ☐

All Lion paperbacks are available from your local bookshop or newsagent, or can be ordered direct from the address below. Just tick the titles you want and fill in the form.

Name (Block letters) ....

Address ....

....

Write to Lion Publishing, Cash Sales Department, PO Box 11, Falmouth, Cornwall TR10 9EN, England.

Please enclose a cheque or postal order to the value of the cover price plus:

UK: 60p for the first book, 25p for the second book and 15p for each additional book ordered to a maximum charge of £1.90.

OVERSEAS: £1.25 for the first book, 75p for the second book plus 28p per copy for each additional book.

BFPO: 60p for the first book, 25p for the second book plus 15p per copy for the next seven books, thereafter 9p per book.

Lion Publishing reserves the right to show on covers and charge new retail prices which may differ from those previously advertised in the text or elsewhere, and to increase postal rates in accordance with the Post Office.